OTHERS SEE US

Grandma's hand trembled as she lit a cigarette, oblivious of the one still burning in an ashtray on her permanently disorganized desk. Did I dare hope she was so bowled over by Annelise's emotions that she might have become forgetful and dropped her guard? It wouldn't be for long. I had to act, and it had to be now.

I was tense as a shoplifter entering a crowded department store; I was cowering with the vulnerability of a dream in which you are naked in a public place and know that in the next instant you'll be caught. But I didn't hesitate. Hoping no alarms would go off, I stepped carefully into Grandma's mind . . .

PUFFIN BOOKS BY WILLIAM SLEATOR

OTHERS SEE US

OTHERS

SEE US

William Sleator

PUFFIN BOOKS

PUFFIN BOOKS
Published by the Penguin Group
Penguin Books USA Inc., 375 Hudson Street, New York, New York 10014, U.S.A.
Penguin Books Ltd, 27 Wrights Lane, London W8 5TZ, England
Penguin Books Australia Ltd, Ringwood, Victoria, Australia
Penguin Books Canada Ltd, 10 Alcorn Avenue, Toronto, Ontario, Canada M4V 3B2
Penguin Books (N.Z.) Ltd, 182-190 Wairau Road, Auckland 10, New Zealand

Penguin Books Ltd, Registered Offices: Harmondsworth, Middlesex, England

First published in the United States of America by Dutton Children's Books,
a division of Penguin Books USA Inc., 1993
Published in Puffin Books, 1995

10 9 8 7 6 5 4 3 2

THE LIBRARY OF CONGRESS HAS CATALOGED THE DUTTON EDITION AS FOLLOWS:
Sleator, William.
Others see us / by William Sleator.—1st ed.
p. cm.
Summary: When an accidental dunking in toxic waste gives sixteen-year-old
Jared the ability to read minds, he discovers horrifying secrets about
family members at the annual summer reunion.
ISBN 0-525-45104-8
[1. Extrasensory perception—Fiction. 2. Science fiction.] I. Title.
PZ7.S6313Ot 1993 [Fic]—dc20 93-18940 CIP AC

Puffin Books ISBN 0-14-037514-7

Printed in the United States of America

Oh wad some power the giftie gie us
To see oursels as others see us!

—ROBERT BURNS

OTHERS SEE US

one

I fell in the swamp on the Fourth of July.

All winter I'd been thinking about my cousin Annelise and looking forward to the summer, when I'd see her again at the family compound on the shore. Then Mom and Dad had to drag me to Europe for the month of June. Castles and restaurants, and all I could think about was Annelise on the beach. We arrived at the compound weeks later than everybody else. The one good thing was that we *had* to get there on the Fourth of July, since Grandma's holiday cookout is the most important event of the summer. We pulled up at our cottage late on the afternoon of the Fourth.

The first thing I always do at the cottage is to hide my journal in its secret place. Then I hop on my old bike and take a ride around the back roads. The bike ride is kind of a ritual with me. I like to get a feel for the place on my own, right away. Even this summer, impatient as I was to see Annelise, I didn't skip the bike ride. There was something delicious about stretching out the wonderful moment just before seeing her for the first time in a year.

I was sixteen and had grown a lot since last summer. My legs were longer and stronger, too, from going out for track. Thinking about Annelise, I kind of got carried away. Pumping up the hills was so effortless that I kept pumping on the way down, too, really working up some speed.

It was too much for the old bike. The brakes went at the bottom of the hill, where the road makes that sharp turn around the swamp, and before I knew it, I was *in* the swamp, up to my ears, gasping and choking at the poisonous chemical stink. It wasn't that long ago that the summer people had finally managed to stop the mill from dumping toxic waste in there, but so far nobody had gotten around to cleaning out all the industrial gunk that had been accumulating in the swamp for years.

It took me awhile to get home, wheeling the clogged bike. Back at the cottage it was embarrassing to admit to Mom and Dad that I had fallen into the swamp. But the stuff was all over me. And anyway I just can't lie, and Mom and Dad and everybody else in the family know it.

Mom didn't want the rest of the family—especially Grandma—to think I was a klutz, so she told me not to mention the swamp accident to anyone else. To be sure no one would notice anything, I had to scrub myself over and over again in the shower in order to get the stink off. Mom and Dad didn't really have to wait for me—it's a short walk over to Grandma's house, the main house right on the beach where all the parties happen—but Mom insisted on hanging around until I was through cleaning up, so she could make sure I got rid of the odor and no one would put me on the spot by asking about it. I was in the shower for a long time.

"You smell like you took a bath in baby oil," Mom commented when I was finally through.

"It helped to dissolve the gunk."

"Well, I *guess* you're presentable enough now," she said, shaking her head and clucking in amusement at my stupidity. She moved toward the door.

That's when it hit me.

A moment later Mom turned back. "Aren't you coming with us, Jared? You're just standing there."

I was just standing there because while Mom had been calmly saying, "Well, I *guess* you're presentable enough now," I heard a kind of ringing in my ears, and my brain was grabbed and shaken by an alien sensation of worry about being late. I had never felt anything like it.

I shook my head. "Uh, I guess I just had some kind of weird déjà vu," I said, blinking.

"Let's go," Mom said.

She and Dad and I strolled together under the big old trees across the lawn, which was dappled with late-afternoon light. The summer estate has been in the family ever since Grandma and Grandpa bought it years and years ago. Mom and her brother and two sisters each have what we call a cottage, though they're more like comfortable houses than cottages, scattered across the property at discrete distances from one another. But none of them is as big as Grandma's old gabled three-story house, with its widow's walk overlooking the sea, which was originally the only building on the place. The big house was impressive but shabby, since Grandma couldn't afford to keep fixing it up. Grandpa died when I was a baby, and Grandma talked a lot about her finan cial struggles since his death; she was always worrying she might have to sell the place.

"Beautiful day for the party," Dad was saying smoothly. Again I was jabbed in the head by a foreign spasm of anxiety, this time about getting enough booze to drink. But I never drank alcohol! The sensation was so intense that I had to make an effort to keep walking and not just freeze again. What was going on? This was getting a little scary.

"Mother gets so much pleasure at having all of us together on these occasions," Mom said. "She's really sentimental at heart." And I was punched by a vivid mental picture of Grandma's face, her bright red mouth twisted in fury as she screamed something extremely nasty at Mom.

"Phew!" I couldn't keep from saying.

Mom and Dad both looked at me.

"My head feels funny," I said uncomfortably, though it wasn't a lie.

"You're sure you didn't swallow any of that swamp stuff?" Mom asked me, for the fifth time. And Grandma's face was replaced by a fearful image of myself lying in a hospital bed covered with pink greasy cancerous lesions.

"I'm sure," I gulped, fighting nausea.

The horrible mental image vanished the instant Grandma's house came into view. The building was a completely different, much lighter color; the entire house had been freshly shingled for the first time in my memory.

Dad raised his eyebrows, and he and Mom exchanged a glance, and somehow I knew they were thinking, *How's the old lady going to keep crying poor after this?* I had never heard them refer to Grandma as "the old lady."

Directly to the right of the house the stone jetty, where boats are moored, extends a hundred yards or so into the water; to the right of the jetty is our private beach. There they all were, amid colorful lawn chairs and umbrellas: Mom's siblings, Maggie and Grace and George, and their spouses and kids, some romping and chasing, others standing and chatting like adults. But it was Grandma who dominated the scene in her oversize Victorian wicker chair, her face brown and leathery, her long white hair streaming down her back, smoke drifting from the cigarette in her hand.

I searched the beach for my first glimpse of Annelise, hoping I wasn't being too obvious about it. Where was she? I remembered she had spent a lot of time with a boy named Bruce last summer.

Waves of heat and delicious smells emanated from the large stone barbecue. Dad—whose name is really Bob, but whom everybody in the family refers to as Bobo—was already moving toward the table beside the barbecue, with its bottles and glasses and ice buckets.

"Elspeth, darling, it's so wonderful to see you!" Aunt Maggie cried, embracing Mom. Mom hugged her back, and then they stood gazing fondly at each other, arms on shoulders.

"What an adorable dress!" Aunt Maggie said. "You look absolutely marvelous!"

Wal-Mart, that dress just screams it.

It felt as though some invisible person had whispered the words into my ear, and I jumped. They were all too preoccupied to notice.

"Don't be silly. You're the one who's never looked better," Mom was saying.

All those new wrinkles. Hasn't she heard of Retin-A?

"Bobo, you're handsomer than ever, with that distinguished touch of gray," Aunt Maggie gushed. "And Jared, you're the picture of your father."

Bobo is so fat! It must be his drinking. And Jared! Who would have believed the little shrimp—always so small for his age—would turn out to be so tall and good-looking?

I managed to mumble appropriate greetings, fighting confusion. What was happening in my brain? Was I going crazy? Trying to appear casual, I shaded my eyes and looked away. And then, briefly, my head cleared. There she was down by the water—Annelise, Uncle George's daughter, only a few months younger than I was. She was playing with Amy, the youngest cousin. It was always someone's responsibility to be with Amy, who had to be watched every minute she was near the water, and Annelise and Amy were especially close.

Annelise turned toward me, shaking back her long, gleaming black hair. Our eyes met. She regarded me blankly for a moment, as though she didn't know who I was. Then her delicate features opened into a smile of amazed recognition. I beamed back at her, glowing inside, automatically starting toward her.

But Mom took my arm. "Come on, Jared," she prompted me, and I was smacked by a jangling, ragged turbulence. "Grandma's waiting."

two

What am I going to tell her about being late? the silent voice was now desperately repeating. It had a nagging quality that was beginning to seem oddly familiar, but I still struggled to push it away.

Grandma looked scrawnier than ever in her loose, peasanty blouse. She didn't get up, of course. She lifted the corners of her lipstick-smeared mouth—its outline jagged because of all her wrinkles—and extended one dark brown arm to touch Mom's cheek and poke Dad in the stomach. Then she looked me up and down appraisingly and finally rested her eyes on mine, her narrow face a relief map of wrinkles. Her smile was still fixed in place, but her expression was unreadable.

"Sorry we're a little late, Mother," Mom began. I almost jumped again. It was startling the way she immediately started talking about what this voice had been whispering into my brain; she had not uttered a word about being late until this moment. "We had some car trouble and just couldn't find—"

Grandma waved her cigarette at her to shush her. "Gee, don't you look swell, boy," she told me in her deep, rasping voice. "Now where did I put my glasses?" She scrabbled around in her bag, found the glasses, slipped them on and studied me again, then nodded knowingly. "I always knew Jared would shoot up overnight," Grandma continued. "I never paid any attention to what Maggie was always saying about what a shrimp he was." She inclined her head toward the drinks table. "Go get yourself some refreshment, Jared. Bobo hasn't hesitated, I see, despite the price of gin. Get something for Elspeth, too." She thrust her plastic glass at me. "And while you're at it, freshen up my G and T, like the dutiful grandson you are."

I took her glass and moved away, thinking about how much I was going to have to write in my journal that night.

Dad was already back at the table, making himself another drink while listening to Uncle George, who was talking about trouble in the neighborhood.

"Nothing like this has ever happened before," Uncle George was saying. "Money's been disappearing from the ATM in town—lots and lots of it."

Five-nine-one-eight, said a voice rather automatically.

Two-six-three-four, said a distinctly different voice.

I finished making Grandma's drink and looked around. Annelise was still playing with Amy, but she noticed as soon as I glanced over there and smiled at me again. How was I going to act cool around Annelise with these voices reciting numbers in my head? I tried not to panic, urging the voices to go away.

"There's no evidence the machine's been tampered with," Uncle George said. "Somehow the thief gets people's cards away from them without their realizing it, and he also seems to know the *numbers* that go with their cards. Money's been vanishing in staggering amounts. There's so much of an outcry, the bank's about to close the thing down. What a pain *that's* going to be."

I fumbled as I squeezed lime into Mom's drink, wondering about Annelise.

"There was also a really peculiar break-in right next door at the Winstons'," Uncle George droned on. "Whoever did it got through the security system without a hitch. The system was apparently in perfect condition, not jimmied with at all. But the alarm didn't go off."

Nine-eight-three-two, said one voice—the same voice that earlier had been worrying about getting enough to drink.

Six-six-eight-one, said the other voice.

"And the crooks didn't take the obvious things like VCRs and PCs," Uncle George continued. "They got into a safe—again, no breakage or tampering—and took personal stuff. The Winstons refuse to say what's missing, like they're *afraid* to mention anything specific. And since they won't say what was stolen, there isn't much the cops can do."

I was now getting the feeling that there was something about the voices that made sense, something that was eluding me. But I was too frazzled to be able to figure it out. I just wanted the voices to stop.

"And then there was that terrible boating accident," Uncle George said, suddenly sounding very somber.

"Yeah?" Dad said.

I was curious, too. But I knew Mom and Grandma wanted their drinks, and I was eager to get to Annelise, and I could find out about this accident later. I made my way back to Mom and Grandma, who thanked me perfunctorily for their drinks and went on with their animated conversation. Grandma had taken up knitting this summer, and she was clicking away with her needles, making something gray and weblike—and doing most of the talking. Mom and Aunt Maggie and Aunt Beatrice, who was Annelise's mother, mostly listened. For once Grandma was not going on and on about how poor she was and how she'd have to sell the place, a topic that usually dominated her conversation. Instead she was expressing her relief that there was no loud music coming from the Winstons next door; we could usually hear it all day on the Fourth of July.

The mental voices and images around Grandma had a different quality from the ones I had picked up when I was with Dad and Uncle George. There was one rather gloating picture of me and how handsome I was, accompanied by an eagerness to bring me back into the conversation. A second voice was concentrating on Lindie, Aunt Maggie's daughter; this voice was itching to switch the subject around to Lindie's acceptance at Harvard. Was one of these voices coming from Mom's brain and the other one from Aunt Maggie's? I didn't want to think about it.

I walked away, stopping briefly to chat with Lindie, noticing, as I always did, her funny New Jersey accent. Lindie grinned at me and seemed pleased when I said something about Harvard. As usual, her manner was bright and jovial. But at the same time I was gripped by a strange and very unpleasant tension. Was I picking up the emotions caused by some secret worry of Lindie's? The idea made me really uncomfortable. I got away from her as soon as I politely could.

But I couldn't get away from what was happening to me. No matter whom I was with, unfamiliar images and emotions kept pouncing into my head. I had to be going crazy, imagining I was picking up other people's thoughts.

And yet . . . some of the stuff I was getting seemed to make a certain sense, to fall into a pattern. But it was too complicated for me to be able to

organize the information while it was actually jumping into me. Tonight, when I was alone, I would
write it all down in my journal and try to make
sense out of it that way. Until then all I could do
was grit my teeth and try to act normal.

But if I *was* picking up other people's thoughts,
then what would Annelise's brain hit me with? I was
apprehensive. I wanted to know what Annelise was
thinking only if what she was thinking was what I
wanted her to think.

But I was still drawn to her. Greeting other people, I worked my way over to Annelise and Amy,
who were building something near the water. Amy
was a cute little kid with white blond hair. As I approached them, everything began to get very much
weirder. The world was turning into a lush animated
cartoon. The sea was too blue to be real, and infi-
nitely inviting. The sand castle they were building
was fantastically elaborate, with impeccably detailed
turrets and balconies. It was perfect, and it would
last forever.

Was this what a five-year-old's brain was like? The
sand castle was really just a blobby wet mess, but
Amy was so enchanted by the structure that it kind
of bothered me to think about how upset she'd be
when the tide rose and wiped the thing out.

"Hi, Jared," Amy said brightly. "Look at our
beautiful castle."

Annelise turned and gazed up at me. I steeled
myself.

And I was splashed by a jubilant heady rush. Was

that how she felt about me? Or was I reading my own feelings into hers? The sensation was too diffuse for me to be sure. Still, I wasn't getting even a hint of anything negative. That was encouraging. Suddenly I *wanted* to believe this fantastic mental ability was real.

Annelise started to get up, and I felt a thrill of excitement from Amy. She longed to run into the magical forbidden ocean by herself; she would head for it as soon as she was left unattended. "Can I help, too?" I said, and quickly knelt beside them. Amy deferred her escape plan, focusing on the castle again, enjoying the attention of two grown-up cousins. Annelise and I patted at the sand as we talked.

We live in Boston; Annelise's family is in San Diego. We never got together during the year. One of the things I enjoyed the most last summer was talking with Annelise. She's very charming and witty, the family favorite. But what I discovered last summer was that we have something special in common. We both want to be writers. She had dropped enough hints to lead me to understand that she kept a secret journal. Though she never directly admitted it, I somehow knew I could trust her and had told her that I myself had a journal that nobody else in the world knew about.

But last summer we had only been friends. Over the year, as I thought about her, my feelings had changed. Even though we hadn't written to each other, knowing our parents would wonder about it, I had been hoping that this summer we could get beyond friendship.

"You had a good year, Jared," Annelise said. "It's written all over you."

"You too," I said, and emboldened by the positive feelings I was still getting from her, I added, "I didn't think you could get any better-looking than you were a year ago, but you managed."

"Oh, come on, Jared," she said shyly, though I knew she was pleased. "So, did you have a nice bike ride?" she asked me; I had told her last year how I always went out on the bike first thing.

I couldn't lie. "Well, not exactly. The brakes failed."

She quickly leaned forward, concerned. "Oh, Jared, you should be more careful on that old thing! I hope you weren't hurt or anything."

"No, I didn't get hurt," I said, and that was the truth. "What's it been like here so far?" I asked her, hastily moving the conversation away from the bike. I didn't want Annelise, of all people, to think I was the kind of stupid and clumsy person who would fall into a disgusting swamp.

"It's been fine. Same as it always is. As usual, the best thing about being here is Grandma, she's such a character." Annelise laughed. "I love the way she puts the fear of God into all her kids, especially my dad. He's so different around her than he is at home, you know what I mean?"

I got a sudden flash of Uncle George as a pompous, domineering bore, who was sometimes rude to Annelise's friends. "Sure I know," I said without thinking. "If he insulted a friend of yours, Grandma would just insult him right back, wouldn't she?"

She stared at me, radiating confusion. "How do you know he does *that*?"

There was no way to answer her. I'd said too much. I realized now I was going to have to be careful with this new skill—if that's what it was—or else I'd be making unexplainable blunders. "Well, I mean . . . um," I said stupidly, knowing that even if I'd been able to think of a lie, I'd never be able to say it convincingly.

"What does *insult* mean?" Amy asked, listening to us now because she could sense something uncomfortable was going on.

"Fix that tower, Amy," Annelise quickly told her, and turned back to me. "I guess I must have said something to you about it last summer," she murmured. "I just didn't expect you to remember. But since you do . . . Well, you can imagine how satisfying it is the way Grandma just effortlessly cuts through Dad's little fixations."

"Fixations?"

"Oh, ever since we got here, all he's been talking about is this supposed *crime* wave," she said. "He always has to have something to worry and lecture people about."

"You mean the stuff about the ATM and the break-in next door? He was telling Dad about it."

She rolled her eyes. "That's exactly what I mean.

Like in less than a minute he's showing off what an authority he is on all the local goings-on."

"Yeah, but that break-in does sound kind of strange."

"You've only heard about it once," Annelise said, with an infectious little chuckle. "Believe me, after listening to him go on and on about it, all you want is to forget the whole thing. 'The Winstons refuse to say what's missing, like they're *afraid* to mention anything specific. And since they won't say what was stolen, there isn't much the cops can do,'" she quoted, imitating Uncle George's voice. "Luckily Grandma's as tired of hearing about it as I am. She changes the subject as soon as Dad brings it up, usually to something outrageous, like how she wants to bomb the Winstons' three-car garage. I love the way she'll just say anything that pops into her mind—things you'd think an old lady like that would never dream of."

"I know," I said. "And she gets a kick out of embarrassing people."

"Embarrassing, embarrassing," Amy chanted to herself, letting wet sand drip through her fingers.

I wanted to keep Annelise entertained, and the way she had described Grandma putting down her father let me know she'd enjoy hearing something similar. "Like what she said about my dad as soon as we got here today," I added.

"Yeah?" Annelise eagerly prompted me, her smile encouraging. "What did she say?"

"She said something about how Dad didn't hesitate to immediately help himself to a drink, despite the price of gin."

"Sounds just like her!" Annelise paused. "Exactly how much would you say your dad drinks every day?"

I was a little shocked. I had assumed Grandma was just teasing. Now I didn't know what to say. Why did Annelise care about the specifics of Dad's drinking behavior? And why, come to think of it, was she so scornful of her own father?

"How much he drinks every day?" Amy repeated.

Annelise laughed warmly. "Can't you tell when I'm joking, Jared?" she said, affectionately pinching my cheek, and I forgot everything else.

Including Amy, who was taking off toward the water. "Amy, come back here!" Annelise yelled, jumping up to retrieve her.

Supper was the traditional steak—blood rare for Grandma—and scalloped potatoes with onions and cheese and a big salad and strawberry shortcake. As the meal ended, I felt oddly fuller than ever before, as though I had eaten my own as well as everyone else's food. And I was besieged by a curious combination of resigned energy stirred together with complacent lethargy. The usual people did most of the cleaning up, and the usual others did their best to avoid it. (Grandma, as she often did at such times, quietly disappeared for a while.) Annelise was one of the most helpful, chattering gaily, making the work enjoyable, thoughtfully fixing Dad an after-dinner drink. Her behavior made Lindie's silent participation seem sullen.

I sensed very strongly how much the family loved Annelise.

After supper there were fireworks on the beach. Annelise moved Grandma's chair for her, made sure Dad had another drink, then sat next to me. I would have liked to slip away with her, but it was too risky. With everyone in the family gathered in one place, our absence would certainly have been noticed. People would wonder what we were doing alone together at night, skipping the fireworks, and our family frowned upon romantic relations between cousins. Other evenings, when there was no official party going on and everyone was dispersed, would be safer.

But it was not easy to be satisfied with just sitting next to her, aware of her happy feelings about me. And I couldn't get any deeper into what she might be thinking; she kept touching my fingers in the sand, and the electric tingle obscured almost everything in my mind.

As soon as the fireworks were over, Uncle George herded his family back to their cottage. With Annelise gone, there was no reason for me to stay around—especially since I was so eager to get to my journal. I was still mystified by what was happening to me and knew that the only way to make sense of it would be to write everything down.

Mom and Dad wanted to stay at the beach a little longer. I excused myself and raced to our cottage. I punched in the security code, 9832, which shut the alarm off for thirty seconds, quickly unlocked the door, and locked it carefully again from the inside. Then I hurried up to my room and to my journal. It was going to take quite awhile to get all this recorded.

Two years ago I had discovered a loose board at the back of my closet, and underneath it a space that was just the right size for my fat spiral notebook. I made sure, when taking the journal out at the end of every summer, to nail the board back in place, so that if people came to do repairs before our arrival, it would not be discovered and replaced by something more difficult to pry open. I lifted the board and reached inside.

The notebook wasn't there.

three

I sank down onto my bed after a frantic search through my room, and Mom and Dad's room, and the rest of the house. It didn't take very long, since we had barely unpacked and there was hardly anything to search through.

The baffling part wasn't that someone had broken into the house; the alarm system was probably malfunctioning. What was impossible to understand was how anyone could have known exactly where my journal was hidden.

At least I was pretty sure Mom or Dad hadn't taken the journal. They hadn't come back from the party yet, and if they'd found it before then—when I was out on the bike or in the shower, for instance—they certainly would have said something about it.

Mom and Dad figured prominently in it, of course. But even when it came to Mom and Dad, I hadn't said anything particularly offensive. There were the usual complaints and descriptions of family squabbles, but most of that stuff they were already aware of. And there was hardly anything in it at all about most of the relatives. I talked about people at school; I wrote stories inspired by my favorite old-time horror movies. No one's feelings around here would be hurt by reading my journal. That wasn't the problem.

The problem was what the journal said about Annelise. I squirmed when those particular entries flashed with appalling, photographic clarity into my mind: my fantasies about Annelise, my very specific remarks concerning her appearance, my attempts at romantic poetry, my secret longings.

If anybody in the family read those things, it would be worse than humiliating; it would destroy any chance of Annelise and me spending time alone together. And right this minute somebody probably *was* reading them.

I found some loose sheets of paper and a pen and began scribbling everything down. Describing the situation and my feelings about it is what I always do when I'm upset about something; it doesn't actually solve the problem, but it usually helps me deal with it.

And tonight it was more important than it had ever been to get my thoughts down on paper. It wasn't just the need to release my anxiety about the missing journal. I also wanted to try to organize the peculiar mental sensations I'd been feeling all afternoon, the invisible voices, the numbers, the alien emotions invading my mind.

But writing about it wasn't working now. I was distracted by the thought that somebody might *read* what I was writing, and that froze me up. After a few minutes I threw down the pen and paper in frustration.

The security alarm went off while I was washing up. I jumped. Then, above its shrill chirping, I heard Mom berating Dad for drunkenly pushing the wrong buttons. The alarm was turned off almost immediately, and as I stepped out of the bathroom, I could hear Mom on the phone, explaining to the cops that it had just been a mistake and wouldn't happen again.

I got into bed with *Anna Karenina*. I loved this book. I was especially impressed by the way Tolstoy seemed to know exactly what was going on in the minds of the characters, all of them so different from one another. But I couldn't concentrate and soon turned off the light, worrying about who had my journal and whether or not I was going crazy.

I felt a little more clearheaded when I woke up the next morning.

OK, maybe reading minds was impossible. But it was also true that a lot of the thoughts I'd been getting had a mundane pettiness—and also a kind of logic—that just didn't seem like hallucinations. My family easily *could* be thinking these things. And if I really had this power to hear their thoughts, then all I had to do to find out who had the journal was to peek into the minds of everybody around me. Maybe when I found the person with the journal, I'd somehow be able to make sure that the thief said *nothing* to anybody else about it.

If it wasn't already too late, that is. I had to hurry. Once news of the journal got around, there'd be no hope of anything happening between Annelise and me.

I stepped into the kitchen and was almost knocked over by a grinding headache and miserably pervasive nausea. I had never seen Dad look so bad; he was obviously the one who felt sick. I stifled my gag reflex and probed a little deeper. And I was amazed by how much my vision had improved overnight.

What I had seen yesterday was like fuzzy silhouettes on a window shade. Today the shade was gone; I could look through the window into the dimly lit interior of Dad's mind. And I could see no inkling of my journal there, only bewilderment about how he had gotten so drunk last night and worries about what he might have said and how much of the evening he had forgotten. It took a little effort, but I found that I was also able to struggle out of his noxious head after I learned what I wanted. I was even able to begin to construct a kind of shield to protect my own brain from his hangover.

Mom, whose brain was not fogged by alcoholic residue, was even easier to read. She was aching with frustration, since she was dying to nag at Dad about how embarrassingly drunk he had been last night—he had never done that in front of her family before—but she didn't want to mention it in my presence. And there seemed to be nothing in her mind about the journal either.

It occurred to me, as I was putting together my usual peanut butter, salami, and cheese sandwich, that I had better tell Mom and Dad that our security system was malfunctioning; whoever had stolen the journal had gotten into the house without setting off the alarm. But in order to tell them, I'd have to mention the journal, and I didn't want them to know about that. It was a real dilemma. I was incapable of lying and saying that something else was missing. At the same time, it was really my duty to inform them about the malfunction. If they didn't get the alarm system fixed right away, other things would probably be stolen, too. My predicament reminded me of something I had heard yesterday, but at first I couldn't think of what it was.

It was not until I had wolfed down the sandwich—it required a certain concentration while I was eating it to maintain my shield against Dad's increased disgust—that the obvious fact finally dawned on me.

There was nothing wrong with our alarm system.

It had worked perfectly when Dad accidentally set it off last night. What was wrong was that *somebody knew our security code*. I sat there, thinking hard, as the situation clarified.

Someone knew the security code for our alarm system. Someone also knew the security code for the Winstons' alarm system, as well as the secret numbers for people's ATM cards. As soon as Uncle George mentioned the robberies yesterday, his and Dad's ATM numbers and alarm security codes flashed instantly into their brains, as easy for me to pluck as ripe tomatoes, except it took me until now to figure out whose voices I was hearing. The more I thought about what Uncle George told us, the more sure I was about how these crimes had been committed— and how my hidden journal had been found.

I was not the only person around who could read minds.

four

"**B**eautiful fireworks last night, didn't you think?"
Mom was saying, making chitchat in front of me while
inwardly brooding about Dad.

"Mmm," Dad said, not wanting to think about
bright, sparkling lights.

I nodded. I was preoccupied by the fact that this
other person with ESP was almost certainly someone
who had been at the party yesterday. Only someone
who had been close enough to me to read my mind
would have known the security code for our cottage

as well as where I had hidden the journal. I had already eliminated Mom and Dad. Uncle George was not a suspect, since he had been so genuinely baffled by the robberies, and neither was Amy. That left me with nine other people in the family to worry about. The only course of action, as I had realized when I woke up, was to go out and directly probe everyone's mind for knowledge of the journal. I had to get started.

"Guess I'll see what's going on down at the beach," I said, getting up.

"Have a good time," Mom said. She eyed me approvingly in my bathing suit. "Just don't get too much sun."

The first person I ran into, before I even reached the volleyball net, was my cousin Eric, Aunt Maggie's son, a year younger than I was. "Hey, Jared."

"Heading for the beach?" I said, digging into his mind.

I barely pushed in the shovel. He was happy to be strolling along beside me, but right underneath that was his panting eagerness to see Annelise. I was stunned. Eric felt the same way about Annelise that I did! He thought about her all the time. And somehow he had gotten the idea she was attracted to him, too. He wanted to—

I instantly backed off, embarrassed, not wanting to be a Peeping Tom. Knowing how Annelise really felt about me, I also felt sorry for the poor guy. This was a lot more awkward than anything I had picked up yesterday.

"Hope you put on some sunscreen," Eric was saying. "The first day I was here I got into a long conversation on the beach and forgot to put any on, and I got burned so bad I was sick," he told me, concerned about my well-being, which only made me feel worse for him. The less I knew about Eric's mind, the better. I had already discovered the only information I needed: Clearly he knew nothing about the journal. If he'd been aware of my feelings for Annelise, which were spelled out on almost every page, it would have hit me the instant I'd taken my first peek into his brain.

"You been following this stuff about the ATM robberies and the break-in and that accident?" I asked him.

He shrugged. "We keep the ATM cards locked up now."

"But what about that break-in?" I asked him. "You can get killed by crazies who break into your house. Doesn't that kind of bother you?"

"The Winstons weren't attacked. Nobody saw a burglar around here. There wasn't any violence. I might be kind of worried if I was afraid of somebody making off with my Macintosh or the VCR. But that's not what was stolen. The Winstons said it was something personal, nothing valuable to anybody else. Who's to say they didn't just lose the stuff themselves?"

"What was the accident?" I asked him.

"Oh." He sighed. "It was awful. A girl named Dee-Dee over on Indian Neck went out in her family's boat alone, and a squall came up, and . . . she drowned."

"Oh, no." What else could I say, since I didn't know the girl? I felt funny talking about it.

We were now close enough to the beach for me to see that Annelise was not there. Her parents, Uncle George and Aunt Beatrice, were heading out to sea in a sailboat. But that wouldn't interfere with my plan. I didn't need to probe Uncle George's mind about the journal, since I was already pretty certain he didn't have ESP, and Aunt Beatrice was almost as unlikely a suspect. And their departure meant that Annelise might be alone in their cottage right now. . . .

Eric was probably thinking the same thing. I didn't check on it, not wanting to invade his privacy. But I still had the advantage; I knew I had to get to her before he did.

"You've got a great body, Jared, but you're white as a sheet!" a hoarse voice shouted from somewhere above us.

It was Grandma, of course, up on the widow's walk with her powerful telescope. One of her favorite pastimes was spying on the neighbors and people cruising by in sailboats and yachts. She had used the telescope so much over the years that she could actually read people's lips with it, even through windows.

"Morning, Grandma!" Eric and I both mouthed back, waving at her. I was also, of course, trying to peek into her head, but she was just too far away up there for me to get anything.

"You start working on your tan this minute, Jared; those are my orders!" Grandma yelled, shaking her bright scarf at me for emphasis. "And keep away from that SPF fifteen sunblock crud. You'll never get anywhere that way. Baby oil's the only thing I ever use. Man, you wouldn't *believe* what's going on in that catamaran out there! Not to mention the *terrible* things they're saying to each other," she added with a guffaw, and grabbed the telescope again.

"She's got a great new 'scope now; you ought to take a look at it," Eric remarked as we turned away.

Aunt Grace and Uncle Ted, the youngest of Mom's generation, were reclining in beach chairs. Amy was digging in the sand beside her parents. I quickly skimmed Amy's mind, just for the cartoonlike fun of it. Amy wanted to be with Annelise, whom she adored more than anyone. And as usual, she was fascinated by the ocean, partly because she knew no one wanted her to get near it. She was quite clever about moving stealthily toward the water. I was good enough now to check people's minds to see who was relegated to keep an eye on Amy. It was her parents, for a change, so I figured she had to be pretty safe.

Aunt Grace and Uncle Ted politely asked me about Europe. I quickly realized that it didn't matter much what I said, since neither of them was really listening to me. Aunt Grace was thinking about her abdominal muscles and her aerobics class. Uncle Ted was thinking about how much younger, better-looking, and more successful he was than Dad—and how pathetically drunk Dad had been last night. Any connection between me and Annelise did not enter their minds. They knew nothing about the journal.

Things were looking up. I hadn't found the other mind reader yet, but news of the journal hadn't spread as quickly as I had feared.

Amy was inching closer to the ocean. If Aunt Grace or Uncle Ted didn't do something, I'd have to bring her back soon.

Then I forgot about Amy, feeling another source of tension. Eric's sister, Lindie, who was a year older than I was and swam vigorously every morning, was just emerging from the water. She was hefty, like Eric and Aunt Maggie and her father, Uncle Eric; Lindie wore a frilly one-piece suit to try to disguise the fact, though it really only made her look bigger.

Lindie quickly wrapped herself in a big beach towel, feeling self-conscious. She was making an effort not to let herself get depressed about the difference between her body and Annelise's. Lindie didn't seem aware that her own face was actually quite pretty and that she had really nice auburn hair. *Harvard, Harvard, I wish Mom would shut up about it, but at least now maybe they think I'm smart and ugly instead of just ugly*, she was firmly lecturing herself, while thinking about holding her stomach in. *And no way are you eating fried clams for lunch again today, just a salad, maybe some yogurt, enough lettuce will fill you up. . . .*

But all this was just on the surface. Underneath I was aware, more than yesterday, that Lindie was struggling with some kind of bleak, pervasive anxiety, more painful than her worries about her self-image. It was something she was making an effort not to think about, to push out of the way, and for that reason—even though I could read a lot more today—I still couldn't get a grasp on it. But I was more curious now.

"You have a great tan, Lindie," I said, in an effort to bolster her self-image, and I was rewarded by a soft and appealing glimmer of pleasure.

In the next second I was hit by Lindie's sharp, envious resentment of Annelise, whom she saw as nasty and calculating. I was shocked. How could brilliant Lindie be so mistaken about Annelise? She was the only person in the family who didn't regard Annelise as an angel.

A moment later I understood. She and Annelise were the only teenage female cousins, and Lindie saw Annelise as someone who had been randomly gifted with great beauty, while Lindie herself had been just as randomly cursed with terrible ugliness. What was so sad was that Lindie had no awareness that she was attractive enough and that people were *not* constantly comparing her with Annelise. There was really no comparison.

I was surprised by the inside of Lindie's mind. I had always known she was intelligent, outspoken, and basically good-natured. Now I was aware of her deep, hidden worry, as well as her more accessible resentment of Annelise and her unrealistically negative self-image. If anybody might pick up any suspicions about Annelise and me, it would be Lindie. But I was already aware that she, too, knew nothing about the journal.

So who did?

Lindie and Eric and I wandered toward the jetty, away from Amy and Aunt Grace and Uncle Ted. "You looking forward to living in Cambridge next year?" I asked Lindie. "There's always a lot of interesting stuff going on there." I lowered my voice. "And you'll be living away from home. I sure envy you for *that*."

"You remember I liked Cambridge when I was there for the interview," she reminded me. "But you can never tell what a place is really like until you're actually living there."

"Don't let her kid you, she's *dying* to get away from Mom and Dad," Eric said, and I knew that was the truth. Then he added mournfully, "And *I'll* be stuck with them by myself."

"You're clever enough to twist them both around your little finger, Eric, my boy," a voice rasped unexpectedly behind us.

We spun around. Grandma had somehow managed to approach us without any of us being aware of it. "You'll never guess what I just found out!" she announced, her excitement making her gasping voice even more breathless than usual. "The Winstons' place is on the market! Not even an exclusive listing—*three* agents have the most garish signs right out in front. Not to mention, I read the lips of the agent who was just showing it when she quoted the price. What would I do without my trusty telescope? The Winstons will be lucky to make half the profit they would have a year ago—if they can unload it at all, that is."

It was an instinct now; I was probing deeply. And all I could find in Grandma's mind was her already very apparent glee—she had despised the Winstons for years—at her neighbors' misfortune. Unlike everyone else in the family, Grandma said exactly what she felt. I marveled at her absolute transparency, reminded of those superinvisible windows that birds are always mashing their brains against. Grandma was the only person I had run across who seemed to have no hidden thoughts at all—no shades, no curtains, not even the thinnest film of dust to let you know a glass barrier might even exist. Everything in her head just spewed right out of her.

"How do you know somebody even worse won't buy the place?" Lindie asked her, sensibly enough.

"Not a chance. Who else would build a three-car garage right on the ocean, in the middle of my view? And that awful music they play!" She grimaced. "*Nobody* could be worse than the Winstons," Grandma affirmed, and in her head there was only total assurance at this prediction.

"I wonder if selling their house has anything to do with their claim that they were robbed," Eric said.

"*Claim* is the word, all right, Eric," Grandma declared, waving her hand with celebratory aplomb.

"I'm glad you're thinking about words. Nothing carries more expression than the right word; Jared can tell you that. The Winstons' maudlin claim was nothing but a pathetic cry for attention, and God knows why they made all that stupid fuss, since its only result will be to bring the price of their house down even lower." And she emitted her characteristic choking cackle.

And then—how had I forgotten for so long?—I thought of Annelise alone in her cottage. I could see her parents still creeping out to sea in their sailboat, tacking laboriously back and forth on this very calm day. There was no way they'd be back in less than two hours.

Eric was thinking the same thing. I didn't have any time to waste. I had to get to Annelise before Eric did.

And then I felt a bright glow of pleasure. It was from Amy, who was heading into the sea. "Hey! Come back, Amy!" I yelled.

Everyone dashed toward her. I was the runner, but it was Lindie, radiating love and panic, who reached Amy first. She lifted her under the arms and carried her gently back to Aunt Grace and Uncle Ted. We all fussed over and chastised her. Lindie was at least as upset as Aunt Grace, and also furious at her, feeling that a negligent mother like Aunt Grace didn't deserve a beautiful child like Amy.

I was worried, too. What would have happened if I hadn't sensed Amy's entry into the water? What if

Lindie hadn't reacted so quickly? Why hadn't Amy's parents been paying more attention to her?

Lindie was the only one who mentioned it. "How did she get so far?" She didn't hide the anger in her voice.

"Oh, you know how she is," said Aunt Grace, not looking at Lindie, toweling Amy off. "You glance away for a second, and suddenly she's just . . . gone."

"Annelise's friend Bruce said I was a real good runner," Amy said proudly.

"Just don't go in the water," Aunt Grace told her.

There was nothing more I could do to help. Amy was OK. Eric and Grandma were calming Lindie down. This was my chance to get to Annelise first. But what if she was with Bruce? I remembered, in a peripheral way, that he was a relative of the Winstons.

"Gee, how long have I been out here without any protection?" I said, moving away from the group. "I better get something to put on my skin right away."

"Baby oil, Jared!" Grandma gasped, pulling a plastic bottle out of her big canvas beach bag and thrusting it into my hand. She looked at her watch. "Hey, I'd better make tracks," she murmured. "Now where did I leave the car keys?" She hurried toward the house.

I took off in the direction of the cottages. As I ran, worried about my journal again, a baffling question occurred to me: Only a mind reader could have stolen my journal, *but why would a person who could read minds go to the trouble of physically stealing something like that?* It would be much easier—and safer—to get whatever you wanted to know directly from the person's mind.

Annelise *was* home alone, it turned out, searching frantically for her journal.

five

I couldn't help reading Annelise's journal.

I wasn't spying; it hit me without warning, before
I could avoid it. She was so alarmed at the possibility that I might have read her journal that she was
mentally broadcasting exactly what the entries contained. And now I could see a lot more clearly into
her mind than yesterday.

"It's just crazy," she kept saying, sitting across
from me on the couch with her hands clasped together. Her long black hair, which was usually per-

fectly groomed, was damply tangled around her face. "No one knew where it was hidden. No one had any idea my notebook might even *exist*—except you." And she studied my face again, chewing at her luscious lower lip.

My first impulse, when she answered the door and I knew at once what had happened, was to tell her right away that my journal had been stolen, too. But I had enough practice now not to make the mistake of reacting to information before it was given to me in words. I asked her what was wrong, I listened, and all the time the contents of her journal splattered and gurgled through my mind like toilet water. I was so stunned by what it contained that I could hardly speak, squeezing the plastic bottle of baby oil in my hands.

April 5

Dear Diary,

Oh, my feelings were so hurt today! I found out that Chuck went to see Alien Headhunters III *with Gail! He thinks she's more fun than me? They think they can sneak around behind my back? They can't think that; nobody can think that. I'll just have to help them understand. I know I can find a way. Sam, who's always looking at me that way, is Chuck's best friend—or at least he has been until now. Wish me luck!*

April 6

Dear Diary,

I was so sweet and charming to Sam today. He's starting to open up already. Keep your fingers crossed!

Dear Diary,

It's working! Sam knows how understanding and discreet I am—and what a good sport I am, how I appreciate boys' type of humor. He loved the way I blushed and giggled when he described the personal things Chuck told the boys in the locker room about Gail, the jokes they made about her. I phoned Gail and helped her out by letting her know. She thanked me, before she broke down and had to hang up.

April 15

Dear Diary,

Congratulate me! It'll be a cold day in August if Chuck and Gail ever speak to each other again—and they're both confiding in me now. Chuck had no idea how paranoid and hysterical she really is; he doesn't know it was because of me that she showed her true colors. Poor, sweet Gail made a lot of slashes around her wrists; too bad they found her in time. Now they've got her on some kind of drug that makes her even dopier than usual; she was always about as bright as that Resussa-Annie doll we use in lifesaving class.

May 3

Dear Diary,

Can you believe? Another stupid scene with poor old Dad—I kept trying not to look at his nose hairs. Same old thing again—too many boys calling me up, me staying out too late. So I told him what I heard Mom saying about him to Hilda on the phone yesterday. That

41

kept them fighting for the rest of the evening and laying off me.

May 18

Dear Diary,

Life is so unfair! No way I can get out of another deadly summer at the beach, a prison there with the boring, ugly old relatives always around and that loathsome nuisance Amy they'll be expecting me to take care of—I wish she'd just drown and get it over with. At least they all realize I'm Miss Perfection. Except for that cow Lindie. Have to figure out some way to get at her. There's also a few other people I can maybe play some cute little tricks on. Like hunky Bruce over on Indian Neck; hunky and rich—they're the most important family in the neighborhood. Hope I won't be saddled with pathetic little Jared; hope the runt won't be tagging along like last summer, interfering. The good news is his family won't be there until July. And maybe I can provide a fun surprise welcome for him that will keep him out of my hair when he does get here. I seem to remember they never bother locking up the shed where he keeps that old bike he's so attached to. . . .

June 5

Dear Diary,

Oh, what a busy, productive day I had yesterday! You would have been so proud of me. My charming conversation kept Eric so fascinated on the beach that he completely forgot about sunscreen. Now Eric's sick in bed, a gorgeous shade of vermilion against those tasteless yellow sheets. Then I decided to create a thrilling adventure for that bleached blond Dee-Dee, who's running after Bruce. All I had to do was let most of the gas out of her family's outboard motor. It wasn't my fault she decided to go out just before that freak squall blew up. Or that the coast guard got to her too late. The bitch shouldn't have gotten in my way. Of course, I made sure to act more upset than anyone else in our family.

July 4

Dear Diary,

I can't wait to tell you! Can you believe Jared is a hunk? If I'd known, I might not have messed up the brakes on his bike. Oh well, he survived. It's going to be a real spicy summer after all. Having Jared to play with, knowing Bruce and Eric are also slobbering over me. It'll be fun sneaking around them and the whole family, too. Like Jared's father—all I had to do was slip him those two extra triples, and he had no idea Jared and I were sitting right there holding hands. And everybody thinks I'm kindly Miss Perfection meaning nobody any harm. Except for that Harvard cow. But you know me. I'll get something on her. She'll learn.

I sat there dumbly, clutching the plastic bottle, my stomach cold. How had I missed so much of what she obviously must have been thinking the day before?

Partly it was that my perceptions had been so hazy then, compared with what I could pick up today. But it also seemed that Annelise really had been impressed by my new appearance. Her powerful involuntary reactions were what I had been aware of yesterday. It must have been later on that the lying, scheming part of her brain took over.

And Lindie was the only one who had seen through Annelise. Not because she was the other mind reader; Lindie knew nothing about my journal. She was just far more perceptive than I had ever realized. She was also honest and tough. It was clear from Annelise's journal that Lindie had not hesitated to let Annelise know, at least since last summer, how she really felt about her.

I was aware of Annelise's cunning now, clicking away underneath her outward panic like a movie projector displaying a horror film. She was interpreting my stupefied behavior as proof that *I* was the one who had taken her journal.

And what made it even more painful was my sharp awareness of how I looked to Annelise at this moment. I wasn't handsome anymore; I was a pale, grublike clod who had stumbled into an intolerable position of power over her. Uppermost in her mind was the craving to wrest this power away from me, after which she would squash me in the dirt like the disgusting oversize bug I had become.

She smiled. And even now her smile wrenched my heart. "All you have to do is give my notebook back, Jared," she said, her voice softly persuasive. "Of course, I'm dying to know how you got in here without setting off the alarm and how you found the hiding place so fast. But that's not the important thing now. What's important is for you to give it back to me right away, like a good boy." She sighed unhappily. "And I thought I could trust you, Jared," she said, sounding wounded. "You know the last thing I want is to tell the whole family how you kept grabbing at me on the beach last night."

"But Annelise, I didn't *take* it!" I said, finally speaking because I just couldn't stand listening to her for another instant.

"Oh, Jared! Nobody but you knows I want to be a writer—or that I might have a notebook with, uh, fictional material in it. And now you're acting like you're afraid I'm going to bite you." There was contempt in her voice. "You think I don't know you, Jared? You can't lie. Guilt's written all over you. You must have done it early this morning when I was helping my parents with the boat. Just go get it now and—"

Suddenly I was angry. "If you're so sure I took your notebook, then maybe you can tell me who stole mine," I interrupted her.

"Huh?"

"My journal was gone when I got home last night. And nobody but you knows about my journal. Not to mention, *I* just got here yesterday. *You've* been around for the last month, while somebody sneaked into the Winstons' house and took their personal papers." I sat back in my chair, staring hard at her. "And you never actually *told* me you had a journal until just now. Think about it. *I* have a lot more reason to be suspicious of you than *you* have to be suspicious of me."

Now she was frightened in a completely different way. Until this moment she had been too upset by the possible exposure of the ugly behavior in her journal to think beyond herself; it had not occurred to her to connect its absence with what was going on in the neighborhood. But she wasn't stupid; she knew that I couldn't lie and that what I was saying made sense.

"It's *not* you? Somebody else has it? And *your* notebook, too?"

I nodded.

"Oh." She paused, thinking for a moment, changing her tactics. "Er, I'm sorry I, uh, got so upset with you, Jared," she apologized. "But I was scared. You don't know what kind of experimental stories I've been writing in that notebook. Fictional stuff. Nobody would understand." She sighed. "Well, at least it's not somebody in the family who has it," she said hopefully. "I mean, if it's the same person who broke into the Winstons', like you said."

"I said maybe. But maybe not." I didn't tell her I knew it *had* to be somebody at the family cookout who had taken my journal because I didn't want to tell her *how* I knew. It was a very good thing I had found out what Annelise was really like before making the mistake of telling her about my new mental abilities.

"Oh," Annelise said again. Then she noticed, for

the first time, the plastic bottle of baby oil I still had in my hands. She smiled, feeling it was the right moment to start being charming to me again. She was masterful, able to pull off this act even though she was still overflowing with anxiety about her journal. "Good old baby oil. Grandma's idea, right?"

"Uh-huh."

She chuckled. "Grandma has this fixation about baby oil," she said.

Her next remark flashed into my mind before she said it in words, but it took me a little longer to begin to grasp its full implication.

"Grandma told me baby oil was the only thing that finally got the gunk off her after she fell in the swamp."

six

I had part of the answer now.

I had begun to pick up people's thoughts—including their security codes—soon after falling into the toxic swamp. Grandma had fallen into the swamp, too. She was always wandering all over the property; no one would think it was odd to see her near either of our cottages.

I now remembered that I had been thinking about my journal—as well as its hiding place—while talking with Grandma yesterday. And today Grandma had made that remark to Eric about words. "Nothing carries more expression than the right word; *Jared can tell you that*," she had said to him. How else could she have known that I *did* think about words if she hadn't peeked into my mind, found out I wanted to be a writer, and also read my journal?

Had Grandma also stolen money from the ATM and broken into the Winstons' house? That was hard to believe. Was there a *third* mind reader around who was the criminal? I still had a lot of questions.

My immediate impulse was to get to Grandma fast.

I cautioned myself to wait a minute, not rush off blindly, construct some kind of strategy first. With Grandma I would have to be very, very careful. If she knew I could read minds, I might never learn anything from her.

Annelise was being outwardly nice to me now, though her worries about her journal continued to dirty the atmosphere, like flies around rotting meat. "What's the matter, Jared? Say something."

I didn't bother to respond, though a corner of my mind registered with pleasure how nonplussed she was that *any* boy could dismiss her with such casual aloofness. I just went on concentrating hard, making an effort to ignore the sharp, painful pinching of her anxiety. I was getting better at shielding my brain from other people's thoughts.

But could I also hide my *own* thoughts from another mind reader? I now knew it must be possible, since Grandma had obviously concealed her real thoughts from me today. But I had no practice at that. How had Grandma done it?

I remembered with a sinking feeling the impossible paradox of the alchemists' formula for turning lead into gold; all you had to do was stir the molten lead while *not* thinking the word *rhinoceros*. What I would have to do to hide my thoughts from Grandma would be a lot harder than that.

Being alone with Grandma would guarantee failure. But filling her mind with distractions from other people might give me somewhere to hide.

What I needed was a diversion so electrifying and magnetic that it would drag the entire focus of Grandma's attention away from me. Knowing Grandma, what would be most irresistible to her would be some deliciously sordid secret.

I was buzzed again by Annelise's swarming insect bites of distress about her journal.

I wasn't as uncontrollably worried about my journal as Annelise was about hers. My emotions had subsided since I'd had more time to adjust to its disappearance. And most of the stuff in my journal was bland and boring compared with the brutal nastiness that dominated Annelise's.

Grandma would certainly consider Annelise's journal a far more toothsome morsel than mine. She had just stolen it this morning and probably hadn't had time to read all of it yet. And Annelise's powerful emotions about her journal were impossible to ignore.

I stood up and looked at my watch. "Meet me at

Grandma's in five minutes," I told her with all the authority I could muster.

"What good will that do?"

"If anybody's read them, don't you think we'll be able to tell? Whoever has them will act different, guilty, something that might give it away." It wasn't a lie; I just wasn't telling her everything.

"But if it *is* that thief in the neighborhood, he won't be at Grandma's."

I wanted her to be as frightened as possible, to attract Grandma's curiosity. "I never said it *couldn't* be somebody in the family who took the journals. Maybe it is. Wouldn't we have noticed somebody else sneaking around here? Anyway, don't you want to eliminate the family as soon as we can? *Nothing* would be worse than one of them finding the notebooks." I paused, and then spoke with grim emphasis. "Until we're sure, we have to consider all our relatives as enemies; we can't stop worrying about any of them for an instant. Don't forget that. Five minutes. Be there."

The first thing I did at the beach was to check on Amy. She was being safely kept away from the water by Eric; Lindie had instructed him not to let her out of his sight for an instant. Not only was Lindie more responsible about Amy than Aunt Grace was, she had been the only one to see through Annelise. Until today, I had been too stupid to notice how unusual Lindie was. Now, eager to find out what other surprises might be in her mind, I was drawn to her.

She was sitting under an umbrella reading *War and Peace*, so it was easy to start a conversation with her about *Anna Karenina*. Annelise's parents were still out sailing, but everyone else was nearby on the beach—except Grandma. I quickly learned from Lindie's mind that Grandma had just returned from some errand; she hadn't said where she had been. Now she was in her study, having mentioned vaguely that she had some kind of business to attend to. While talking to Lindie, I hopped from one mind to another, looking for more information about Grandma. I knew by now that trying to read several minds at once was confusing, like trying to listen to two different radio stations. You learned a lot more by focusing on only one mind at a time.

No one knew what Grandma's errand had been. And many people were curious about what she was doing inside, since Grandma's usual pattern was to inflict upon her skin the sunlight of midday, when the rays were most dangerous. Getting the deepest possible tan as quickly as possible was not her only motivation; everyone knew Grandma enjoyed flaunting her utter disregard of the family's disapproval, since the more they begged her to be careful about the sun, the darker she got.

And now Grandma probably also got a tremendous charge out of looking into the minds of her children and their spouses and learning which of them were genuinely concerned about her health and which were *hoping* she would die of skin cancer, the sooner the better.

Grandma had always claimed that she had serious money problems, constantly threatening that she was going to have to sell off portions of the estate, if not the whole thing. But despite what Grandma said, it was no secret that all her offspring and their spouses believed her death would result in inheritances for them. That was probably the main reason Grandma had always relished going on and on about how she really had no money at all.

But this year, for the first time in all my memories of her, Grandma had not said *one word* about how poor she was.

I forgot about it as soon as Annelise arrived. Her dark hair was brushed and gleaming again, as straight and perfect and boring as a wig on a department store dummy. She was calm and poised, despite the specific thoughts about her journal that were stinging me like hungry flies, accompanied by her feverish plotting of potential defense strategies. She squatted down beside me and Lindie as casually as if nothing were the matter at all.

It was interesting to see them together, reading Lindie's distaste for Annelise's falseness, her envy at Annelise's beauty. Sure, Lindie needed to lose a little weight. But her curly, tousled hair was actually much prettier than Annelise's. I was more curious than ever about the terrible worry that gnawed at Lindie, which was now just inches beyond my reach.

But I had no time to think about that now. I had to get Annelise and Grandma and me together. "I'm going in to get something to drink." I tilted my head at Annelise and stood up.

"Me too," Annelise said. "You want anything, Lindie?"

Lindie shook her head silently, not thanking Annelise, and turned back to her book.

Annelise didn't know why I wanted to go inside, but she felt so self-conscious about confronting anybody who might have seen her journal that she was grateful for the chance to avoid the relatives for as long as possible.

We went in through the side door, which leads into the kitchen; the ancient patched screen had been replaced by a sturdy new one. It was cool and dark inside, and there was a faint garbagy smell, with dirty dishes and old newspapers all over the place. I knew where Grandma's study was, at the opposite end of the house from the kitchen, but I stalled in front of the shiny new refrigerator.

I was very nervous about facing Grandma. It seemed of utmost importance to me that Grandma mustn't know yet that I could read minds, too. If she knew, she'd keep everything important from me; I'd never find out about the journals or be able to use my abilities to get them back.

Grandma had to know that the thief in the neighborhood had fallen into the swamp and could read minds. That was why she had set up the barrier yesterday, in front of all the others, that gave the impression there was nothing in her mind but what she was verbalizing. But Grandma had no reason to be suspicious of my being a mind reader, since the crimes had taken place before my arrival. My hope was that with only Annelise and me around she would let down her guard, distracted by Annelise's stinging thoughts, and give me a chance to peek inside hers.

But she would never do this if she had an inkling of what I could do and what I knew about her. So how was I going to *not* think about those things?

One strategy might be simply to focus my attention on the objective world—the spiderwebs in the corners, the linoleum on the floor, the views through the dusty windows—giving Grandma nothing interesting but Annelise's mind to pick up. I was pretty sure she'd be hooked by Annelise's insidious intensity, her fears, and her plotting as soon as she got a sniff of them. And I knew you picked up more if you concentrated only on one mind at a time, meaning Annelise's thoughts might keep Grandma away from mine.

"Let's go tease Grandma about her tan fading," I said.

"Huh?" Annelise wasn't suspicious of Grandma.

"Lindie told me she was in her study. Maybe she's *reading* something," I said in a significant whisper, staring hard at Annelise.

Annelise's eyes widened as for the first time she connected Grandma with the journals. Annelise knew very well how much Grandma adored gossip and relished speaking her mind. Her horror boomed and ignited with the fury of an incendiary bomb. I ducked away from the raging bonfire, actually breaking into a sweat from the intense heat.

"But—but what will we do if she *has* them?" Annelise had no idea that to a mind reader, her uncontrollable speculation about exactly what Grandma might have read was exactly like searchlight beacons splaying the contents of her journal across the night sky.

"If she's read them, that's all the more reason to stop her—now."

Annelise couldn't argue with that. She reluctantly followed me out of the kitchen, past the stairway piled with objects that were never carried upstairs, down the dark, narrow hallway. I paused outside the closed study door.

How much power did Grandma really have? What if I couldn't hide from her? What would she do to me if she found out what I knew about her?

My worries were interrupted—again—by Annelise's hot, glaring klieg lights of distress. I held my breath and knocked on the door of Grandma's study.

"Who's there?" Grandma called out, and I heard papers rustling, a drawer slamming shut.

"Jared and Annelise," I answered. "We missed you outside. Are you OK?"

"Well, aren't you sweet, worrying about your poor old grandma!" More hurried shuffling. "Come in, come in."

Her study was a small dark room that reeked of cigarette smoke. As I stepped inside, I concentrated on the old library table piled sloppily with magazines and papers, the cobwebs on the green-shaded lamp, the yellowed photographs glued haphazardly to the dirty walls. I did what I could to keep away from Annelise's mind-scorching conflagration.

Grandma actually flinched, not prepared for anything of such violence, her blotchy red mouth twitching in an odd sort of way, her eyes instantly riveted on Annelise.

"Aren't . . . you . . . afraid . . . your . . . tan . . . will . . . fade?" I managed to utter, my voice flat and unconvincing as I struggled to concentrate on a decades-old photograph of Grandma and Grandpa. I was pretty sure that Annelise's adrenaline rush was beating through Grandma with the force of an amplifier at a rock concert. Unaware of the possibility of mind readers, Annelise was doing nothing to censor the contents of her mind.

Grandma was good, all right. She quickly covered her reaction, putting down her knitting, forcing a smile, pushing her glasses up on her nose, her ironic tone convincingly normal. "You should talk, still pale as a jellyfish, ignoring your grandmother's instructions," she chastised me.

But Grandma's hand trembled as she lit a cigarette, oblivious of the one still burning in an ashtray on her permanently disorganized desk. Did I dare hope she was so bowled over by Annelise's emotions that she might have become forgetful and dropped her guard? It wouldn't be for long. I had to act, and it had to be now.

I was tense as a shoplifter entering a crowded department store; I was cowering with the vulnerability of a dream in which you are naked in a public place and know that in the next instant you'll be caught. But I didn't hesitate. Hoping no alarms would go off, I stepped carefully into Grandma's mind.

seven

A whirling tunnel of dark, abstract shapes almost knocked me off my feet. I staggered to maintain my balance against the pitch and yaw, a passenger on a storm-racked ship. There was no barrier, no wall of superficial thoughts that had shut me out before.

Compared with this, reading an ordinary person was like a muffled phone conversation with a few pictures and noises in the background. Grandma's mind seemed to be an entire world. I was scared, because it was so hard to interpret the shifting kaleidoscopic images in this crazy place. Yet somehow I *did* know there was no awareness of my presence. I had made it inside!

I tried to stifle my elation; an emotional outburst like that could instantly expose me. Remaining hidden here required rigid discipline, a quelling of all feeling, a cloak of numbness and silence. The slightest misstep in this mine field would detonate a bomb, revealing my presence.

And at the same time I had to pay attention to what Grandma and Annelise were saying.

"If Jared tried to get a tan on the first day, he'd just get horribly burned, you know that, Grandma." Annelise was trying to convey concern for my welfare. "It can really be dangerous."

I began to see that there were already bombs going off in Grandma's mind—apparently her perceptions of Annelise's mental fireworks and planned verbal defenses—which were probably what was keeping me hidden. My strategy seemed to be working, at least for now: Grandma was ignoring my mind and focusing her full attention on Annelise. I hoped Annelise's violent thoughts would continue to camouflage me for a long time. It was going to take awhile to learn anything in here.

I had read that when people who have been blind from birth are given sight, their first perceptions of the world are meaningless to them. Ignorant of the language of vision, all they see are incoherent patterns. It takes them awhile to acquire the skill of translating these abstractions into images that convey useful information. Entering the brain of another mind reader like Grandma was much the same for me.

"OK, OK," Grandma responded to Annelise. "But please do me a favor and don't start lecturing me about skin cancer like your boring parents. That can't be what you came in here to talk about."

I concentrated. A picture began to form, swirling particles gradually stabilizing. It was like beginning to see what's really going on in a splotchy impressionistic painting.

I was in a midnight forest, moving through the mist and the trees toward a warm light. I could hear Annelise's bombs like thunder in the distance. The ground was uneven, but I couldn't risk falling, or Grandma might notice me. Don't cling, don't grasp, touch delicately, delicately, I whispered to myself, stumbling. I reached the thick stucco wall of the cottage. I peered into the deeply embrasured window.

"Of course not, Grandma," Annelise was saying. "I think your tan looks great."

Firelight flickered over the beamed cottage ceiling. My vision expanded, like a camera coming into focus. Warm peasant rugs on the floor; beautiful woven tapestries on the walls; soft, inviting furniture piled with homespun cushions. I longed to go inside—especially because I suddenly noticed a bookcase and table in the corner. But could I really get this far—into the coziest place I had ever seen—without Grandma noticing it?

Grandma shrugged, pulling her glasses off and

tossing them onto the cluttered desk. She flicked cigarette ashes onto her blouse. "Thank you, dear," she
said dryly to Annelise, her eyes fixed on her. "By
the way, you know the Winstons put their house on
the market? Your friend Bruce must know something
about it. He's their nephew, and his family practi-
cally runs the neighborhood."

Annelise's reaction to this remark set off another
roll of thunder; she obviously didn't want Bruce
mentioned in my presence. Grandma's cottage beckoned me. I hoped the thunder was loud enough to
cover the sound of my knees scraping on the win-
dowsill, my feet dropping lightly onto the floor.

I was inside Grandma's inner house. I stood without moving, waiting, in the orderly, spanking-clean
room. There was still no awareness of my presence,
no alarms going off, no sudden change at all. I heard
the hiss of the fire and, from another room, a faint
pleasant clacketing sound, like someone operating an
old-fashioned mechanism.

I took a careful step, then another. Everything
kept getting clearer. I felt the thick rugs under my
feet, I was aware of the intricate patterns woven into
the tapestries on the walls. I reached the large table.
There was nothing as obvious as our notebooks
there. But there were other notebooks, and papers
and envelopes, all meticulously arranged. Holding
my breath, I picked up one of the papers.

"I don't know what Bruce knows. I haven't seen
him for a while. He's kind of boring." Annelise spoke

offhandedly, continuing to behave normally on the surface.

But the furor was still going on inside her, lightning flickering in the sky outside the cottage. Grandma must be glancing at the sky from another window while she was working; I sensed that it was Grandma who was operating the clacketing device I could hear in the other room.

Even though she seemed to be occupied, I still had to hurry. There was no way Grandma would ignore me for much longer. In a moment she'd leave Annelise—fascinating as she was—and peruse my mind. I had to get out before she did that, or she'd catch me.

But first I *had* to find out if she really did have the journals. I poked around the desk, reading neat lists of things—yarn, dyes, other weaving equipment—trying to put everything back in its exact place. And then—my vision constantly improving—I became aware that one volume in particular seemed to pulse with life, with emotion. I picked it up.

"You're not saying much, Jared. What's on your mind?" Grandma said, leaning toward me, her elbows on her desk, among overflowing ashtrays and crushed cigarette packs and her momentarily discarded knitting.

"Uh . . ." It was an effort for me to respond to what was going on in the outside world. "I was just thinking about how . . . how Amy said Bruce told her she was a good runner—after she almost made it into the ocean today," I managed to say, hoping Annelise's discomfort with the subject of Bruce would keep Grandma fixed on her a little longer.

It seemed to work. Grandma had been on the verge of picking up my brain like a magazine at the checkout counter, but my mention of Amy and Bruce sent her back to Annelise.

I quickly opened the glowing notebook. It was a photograph album. Nervous about being caught, I flipped the first pages hastily, old photographs, when Grandma and her children were young.

Then I began to notice something very peculiar about the photographs and turned the pages more slowly. As Grandma's children grew older, into adulthood, their pictures shifted back and forth, changing from the way they really looked into almost monstrous images. Was this Grandma's real opinion of them? Uncle George was corpulent with greed, Aunt Grace gnawing away at her own body with self-absorption. Aunt Maggie, surprisingly, was almost emaciated, but that was because she never stopped running, always trying to keep ahead of everybody else. I was offended by the picture of Mom as a fluffy little lapdog with no mind of its own.

Suddenly I noticed that the clacketing noise had stopped. And then I heard approaching footsteps.

"I'm so worried about Amy," Annelise said, sounding quite sincere.

But Grandma was no longer interested in Annelise. She was after me now.

I flipped frantically through the album. I had to

find the answer, after getting this close. I might never have another chance.

And then there was a photo of me and, across from it, a photo of Annelise. They shifted. And I knew that Grandma *had* read the journals.

The footsteps stopped just outside the door; I heard the doorknob turn. I dropped the photo album on the cottage table. I had no time to close it or put it back in its place. I turned and fled through the window and burst into Grandma's untidy study just as the footsteps entered the room.

But I wasn't safe. I had just been in Grandma's mind. Grandma, entering mine, would see what I knew. I struggled to avoid thinking about these things—just as I had avoided Dad's hangover at breakfast.

And I had another defense. I concentrated hard on exactly what I had written in my journal, imitating Annelise's panic reaction, hoping to blot everything else out.

Grandma nodded. "I know how very devoted to Amy you are, Annelise dear. Now where did I put my glasses?"

"They're right there on the desk," Annelise told her.

"Oh, that's right." Grandma found the glasses and slipped them on. For a long moment she sat there staring at us, her head tilted thoughtfully to the side, her long, thin hair trailing white over her blue blouse.

I concentrated on my journal. I was sweating with the effort it took *not* to think about Grandma's mind. It was the most difficult thing I had ever done.

What made it so hard was that now I *wanted* Grandma to know I could read minds, too. I had seen the cozy welcoming warmth of her cottage, her true inner self. It was only some kind of innate caution, some self-protective mechanism that I didn't understand, that kept me from telling Grandma all the secret information about my own mental powers.

Being a reader, Grandma would have known all about Annelise even before reading her journal. And the picture of Annelise in her mental photo album showed me that she was worried that Annelise would play more of her dangerous tricks on me. She saw Annelise now as a hungry parasitical worm, feeding on others.

I, on the other hand, was better-looking in Grandma's photograph than I was in real life. She was on my side, a deeper friend and ally than I had ever imagined. If I let her know everything, she would be able to help me more than anyone else in the world.

So why wasn't I opening up to her? Why was I paying any attention to that paranoid nagging warning to watch out? It was like a fragile, overinflated balloon, holding in my secret.

But in the instant before I popped it, Grandma spoke.

"Actually, it's adorable that you two came in here together just now," she said, her eyes moving quickly back and forth between Annelise and me. "I'm impressed with you both. Your journals are better written than I expected."

Annelise and I turned to each other, equally stunned, though for different reasons.

"Just the right moment for a little chat," Grandma went on, so interested in observing our reactions that she wasn't even lighting another cigarette. "Nothing to worry about, really. You two will enjoy my terms. And once you've done what I want . . . then no one else will need to read your journals."

Now I understood the balloon that had warned me *not* to give my secret away to Grandma.

I had wondered before why a person who could learn people's secrets by reading their minds would go to the trouble and risk of physically *stealing* their journals.

Now I knew.

eight

"**H**ow did you find them? How did you even *know* about them?" Annelise whispered, her face pale despite her permanent California tan.

"Tut-tut, child. You needn't be concerned about those trivialities. Just do your grandma a little favor and you'll have your journal back in a jiffy."

"I don't know anything about Jared's, but my notebook isn't a journal, Grandma," Annelise said, flinging up a protective scaffolding with her usual speed. But this situation was so extreme that her little laugh was unconvincing. "It's a novel I'm working on. You thought it was real? I'm so flattered! I had no idea it was that good."

Grandma beamed admiringly at her. "Well, I guess there's no reason for me not to show it to your parents then, is there? Just think how proud they'll be to find out about their little girl's literary skills."

Annelise's scaffolding swayed, great sections toppling. "I know you're just teasing us, Grandma. You'd never do anything like that. You're just . . . I mean . . ."

"Of course I won't let them see it, darling," Grandma soothed her, pursing her lips sympathetically. "It hurts me to see you upsetting yourself so. Believe me, I'll give it right back to you—"

"You *were* just teasing! I knew it!" Annelise cried, clasping her hands together.

"—as soon as you complete your amusing little task," Grandma finished. "Nothing to it at all, I promise you." She turned away to light a cigarette.

It was hot in the small room. A spider was busily weaving a web on Grandma's lamp shade, moving toward Annelise, who shifted her chair away from it. A clock ticked. Voices outside shouted happily over the rumbling surf.

"What do you want, Grandma?" I said softly.

"Good boy, Jared," she complimented me, blowing out smoke. "Getting right to the point without shilly-shallying around. It shows up in your writing, too; your directness and economy of style are most impressive." She waved her hand; ashes spilled all over. "One entry in particular about certain fantasies I found especially . . ."

But *she* wasn't getting to the point; she was intentionally avoiding telling us what she wanted, taking pleasure in prolonging our discomfort.

I was still managing to keep my mind securely ignorant. I honestly had no idea why she needed *us* to help her; my curiosity about it was so overwhelming it helped me bury and disperse my newly discovered information about Grandma, knowledge that would have exposed my powers to her. I was really getting the knack of how *not* to think about specific things now. Only later, safely away from her, would I allow myself to snap all the pieces together.

Grandma had moved on to Annelise's "novel." "Your manuscript is such a convincing depiction of an utterly amoral, manipulative person, totally self-involved, with a chilling lack of any concern for the feelings of others. A real literary achievement, my dear, especially coming as it does from such a sweet and thoughtful child as yourself." Grandma smiled lovingly at her. "I'm so impressed with all your hard work, Annelise. Clearly it must have taken a great deal of research in psychology texts for you even to be able to conceive of such a character, let alone portray her so realistically. Jog my feeble old memory, darling. I know the psychologists have some term for the serious—but often undetectable—mental problem your imaginary protagonist suffers from. 'Sociopath,' 'narcissistic character disorder,' something like that. Is it one of those, dear?"

"Er . . . um, I think so," Annelise managed to mutter.

"What do you want us to do, Grandma?" I said.

"Oh, *that!*" Grandma opened her spidery, thin arms with a casual shrug, as though her motive for blackmailing us was far less important than this discussion of our literary talents. She concentrated on stabbing out her cigarette. "It's just that they've finally gotten around to dredging out that toxic waste dump, thank heaven. The fence went up today, sooner than I expected. It's all terribly hush-hush; they don't want anybody to get near the place."

I could only hope that Annelise's utter bafflement was strong enough to be more noticeable to Grandma than the revelation it was now quite a struggle for me to keep wrapped up and out of sight.

"You're talking about that old factory swamp you fell into last month?" Annelise said, her features twisted in puzzled disgust.

"Such an embarrassing experience *that* was!" Grandma exclaimed, pausing to cough briefly. "I had such a time getting out. I'd feel like an old fool going near that place again. Not to mention I'm too old to climb over that fence—especially in the middle of the night. But the two of you together, so young, in such good shape. I know you won't have any problems. I'll provide you with everything you need."

"I still . . . don't understand what you're asking us to do, Grandma," I said.

"I thought it would be amusing to keep a sample, you know, a kind of historical memento, that's all."

She shrugged again in an attempt to convey once more that her request was a mere trivial whim. "A half gallon will be plenty. Nothing to it, really. OK?" she said brightly, nodding, smiling, picking up her knitting. "You give it to me, I give you your notebooks. Agreed?"

nine

"The old lady's completely out of her mind, se-nile," Annelise whispered in the dark hallway, the study door closed behind us, our interview with Grandma over at last.

"She has our notebooks," I said, wondering how far I had to be from Grandma before my mind would be protected by distance. Hiding my thoughts from her had been like holding my breath underwater; I was dying for a gasp of air.

"But it's just so *crazy!*" Annelise was making an

effort to keep her voice down. "Going to all that trouble, stealing our notebooks, blackmailing us—because she wants some of that *swamp* water?"

It only made sense that Annelise would see our task as senseless, incomprehensible. And I knew I must *not* give her any reason to think otherwise. I shook my head and sighed. I couldn't lie, even to someone like Annelise, but that didn't mean I had to tell her everything. I just wanted to run from the house and let my stifled thoughts out. "You know Grandma's always been an oddball."

"That's for sure," Annelise muttered, giving me a sidelong glance. Of course, the worst thing for her would be for her parents to see her journal, but she was also worried about my getting an inkling of its contents. She assumed I was curious; she wondered how much I might have guessed from what Grandma had said about it. "The crazy things she imagined about my . . . uh, novel were just as out of touch with reality as everything else she was talking about," Annelise said earnestly as we entered the kitchen. "She's really losing it. All these yucky spiderwebs!"

"Mmm," I said.

She stopped, suddenly grabbing my arm. "You think we can trust her? What if we do what she wants and she *still* doesn't give them back?"

I had to get out of Grandma's range fast; the balloon that had protected me before was about to burst. "I don't think she'll do that." I tried to sound sure of myself, wanting to howl with impatience. "I mean, she knows *we* don't care about that swamp water. All we have to do is show her she has to hand over the journals first or we'll throw it away. She knows we have no reason to double-cross her. Doesn't that make sense?"

"I guess so," Annelise said, puzzling it over with maddening slowness. She knew Grandma was clever. Grandma had gotten her hands on the journals; she knew exactly how to manipulate us. Despite what Annelise had been saying, she did not believe Grandma was totally out of her mind. She was even wondering if there really *might* be something special, precious even, about the swamp water.

The value of the swamp water was the last thing I wanted Annelise to suspect. Grandma's assessment of Annelise had been right on target. She was already cruel and amoral, delighting in hurting others. Given the power to read minds, she'd be a monster. I tried to assure myself there was no way Annelise could figure out what the swamp water actually did.

But what if she fell in the swamp?

It would be dark out there, it was slippery, the fence might be very close to the water. . . .

I was sweating profusely now, my unleashed thoughts battering at my skull more painfully than Dad's hangover. "Listen, Annelise. That swamp water must be pretty disgusting," I began.

"How do you know?" she asked, eyeing me curiously.

I clenched my fists. I couldn't tell her I had fallen in; then she'd be even more curious about why I had kept it a secret from her and from Grandma. "It's toxic waste, isn't it?" I impatiently demanded. "Toxic waste is disgusting—and dangerous."

"Then why does Grandma want it?" Annelise said, frowning, thinking hard.

"You said she was crazy," I argued, with difficulty. The blood vessels in my face were dilating with the intense effort of smothering my real thoughts about Grandma. "I mean, I don't want you in any danger, being exposed to it or anything. So I was just going to say I'd be willing to get the stuff myself, if you're afraid."

A wrong move, made out of desperation and because of the distracting agony of squelching my thoughts for so long. I had succeeded only in making Annelise suspicious—and more curious. "Gee, how thoughtful of you, Jared," she said with a cool smile. "But I think I'll go along just the same. I'm not chicken. I like the idea of doing something kind of wild. Anyway, Grandma wants us *both* to go. If I didn't help, too, I might not get my notebook back."

I couldn't keep this up for another instant. "Sure, Annelise. Just an idea. I'm going outside. They'll start wondering why we were in here for so long."

I put my hand on the door, turning from the dark kitchen toward the brilliant sunlight, unleashing my thoughts at last.

The new telescope, the screen door, the expensive

shingles on Grandma's house, the sparkling refrigerator, Grandma saying nothing this year about how poor she was.

She had somehow gotten her hands on people's cards and stolen money from the ATM. She had blackmailed the detested Winstons next door, forcing them to put their house on the market when prices were way down. How soon would Grandma—with plenty of stolen money at her disposal—grab up the property?

Grandma had said she had trouble getting out of the swamp; it had taken me only seconds. She had been exposed to the water longer than I had. Her powers must be greater than mine. It scared me, knowing how ingenious and cold-blooded she was, to think of how closely I had come to being discovered inside Grandma's mind. What would she do if she ever caught me?

And what had I learned by taking the enormous risk of going in there? Only that she was the one who had our journals, which she had told us anyway almost as soon as I got out.

No, that wasn't all I picked up. I had learned something else, something that might be very important. Things might not be so bad after all.

Because I had also seen, in the clean and cozy and inviting cottage of her mind, Grandma's magic photo album. The photo of me was handsome and virtuous; Annelise was a slimy object of horror. To Grandma, Annelise was the ruthless enemy, I was the good-

hearted innocent she wanted to protect. I had felt
this so strongly from Grandma it had almost seduced
me into revealing myself to her.

I still had a lot of questions; I was still in danger.
But perhaps not as much danger as I had thought a
moment ago. It *had* been worth the risk to find that
out. Grandma was unscrupulous, but she might not
be a total villain. The benign atmosphere of her secret cottage proved that, didn't it? She cared about
some people, at any rate, and I seemed to be one of
them.

It was Annelise who cared about no one, Annelise
who would be the real danger if she gained access to
the swamp.

The screen door thudded behind us. Mom and Dad
were nowhere in sight, Annelise's parents still apparently out in the sailboat. The others were packing up
from the beach for the move toward their cottages
for lunch.

Aunt Maggie glanced toward us. "Your parents
seem to have deserted you, Annelise," she called out.
"You and Jared want to have a sandwich with us?"

"I'll go out for fried clams," Eric eagerly offered.
He was dying for Annelise to have lunch with them.

Lindie was vigorously shaking sand out of a beach
towel. Hefty she might be, but there was no jiggle of
flab. Swimming had done her good; her movements
had the brisk efficiency of an athlete, a refreshing
contrast with Annelise's self-conscious slouch as she
sidled past me, brushing away a fly. "Sure, thanks a

lot, I adore fried clams," Annelise said, smiling so sweetly, basking in her power as Eric happily blushed.

Lindie noted Annelise's slouch, aware that it was intentionally provocative. But it did not occur to her that any *male* might not be taken in by it or might see Lindie as in any way appealing in comparison.

Lindie did not want Annelise or me in their house; she did not want to be confronted by my typical male adoration of Annelise as much as she did not want to be confronted by fried clams. Confining herself to lettuce would be even more difficult under our pitying gaze. But she couldn't gracefully prevent us from coming. She was trying, instead, to figure out how to absent herself from the meal in some natural, unnoticeable way.

She was also aching with that other, deeply hidden worry. I was on the verge of focusing in on it now. My exploration of Grandma's mind seemed to have enhanced my powers considerably.

"Don't get any fried clams for me," I said. "My track coach says they're a no-no. I'll just have a salad at home."

Lindie was surprised at my interest in salad. But what really impressed her was my refusal of an offer to have lunch in Annelise's presence. It occurred to her for the first time that I might not be Annelise's usual dupe.

And at that moment the hard shell that was hiding her worry from me softened, and I reached in and pulled it out: Lindie had cheated to get into Harvard.

I couldn't read all the details. It had something to do with her math SATs. Her family lived in New Jersey, where the tests were made, and she had managed to get a copy of the test in advance from someone called Zippy. Math was her worst subject. She had been terrified that a low score would ruin her chances, and she had done this rash thing. It had been too tempting to resist.

The simple fear of getting caught was only part of what tormented her. What she found really intolerable was that she had cheated at all. In her eyes, it made her more despicable than anyone else in the family—even Annelise. And it also increased her determination to be as honest as possible about everything else.

But she wasn't consciously thinking about all this right now. She smiled at me as she finished folding the towel. "We have plenty of salad stuff, Jared," she said.

"Okay. Thanks," I said, smiling back at her. And all at once I looked forward very, very much to having lunch with Lindie. I simply wanted to be with her. Eric and Bruce and every other boy in the vicinity were welcome to Annelise. My only concern about Annelise was how to keep her out of the swamp.

I was aware now that Annelise couldn't stand the way I was smiling at Lindie. Annelise already had Eric and Bruce; she saw me as a contemptible slug. Yet Annelise interpreted any attention I paid to Lindie as a brutal slap in the face to herself. Admiration from others was an addictive drug to her. She *had* to have it. She was a lot sicker than I had realized.

But Grandma must have known.

Why on earth did Grandma want *Annelise* to get anywhere near the swamp?

ten

Grandma had given us detailed instructions.

I lay miserably in bed in the dark while the illuminated dial on my wristwatch crawled so slowly toward 3:00 A.M. I itched to get up and pace but knew that might keep Mom and Dad awake, and they had to be so deeply asleep that they would not hear me leaving the cottage.

I worried about Annelise falling in the swamp. I thought about how surprisingly much I liked Lindie.

I wondered what was really going on in Grandma's mind.

At quarter to three it was physically impossible for me to wait any longer. Mom and Dad had to be asleep by now, and the hum of the air conditioner in their bedroom would mask any sound I might make. I pushed the sheet aside and carefully sat up, wincing as the bed squeaked. My eyes had long ago adjusted to the darkness; it took me no time to lace up my sneakers and slip on my backpack.

I clicked my bedroom door softly behind me. The upstairs hallway was small; I was close enough to reach out to Mom and Dad. I didn't get much from Dad, except that he was deeply asleep. But Mom's mind was the first glimpse I'd had of another person's vivid dream. She was running desperately through the crowded streets of Florence, trying to find me, a helpless five-year-old lost in the milling throngs of tourists. I had always known she loved me and worried about me, but I had never before felt with full force the fearfulness and vulnerability of her maternal instincts. I was moved and guilty and also repelled. She was asleep, that was all I needed to know, and I got out of her dream fast.

I wished I could escape the house as easily. Slowly, slowly I descended the stairs, my hand on the wall. At the faintest creak of a floorboard I froze, reaching back into Mom's mind like an air traffic controller checking flight patterns and weather conditions. She was now in Paris. Dad was at the top of the Eiffel Tower, leaning unsteadily over a balcony with me in his arms. Mom was at the bottom, waiting in a frenzy in an endless line for the elevator. I was so disturbed by her anxiety that I scooted from the bottom of the stairs and grabbed the front doorknob without thinking.

It was only muscle memory that reminded me of the alarm in time. I quickly switched it off, unlocked the door, stepped outside, then forced myself to take the time to pull the door shut silently, sure it was taking more than thirty seconds and the alarm was about to sound. But my time sense was distorted by nerves; I reset the alarm with fifteen seconds to spare.

I was safely out of the house but still as tense as before. I wouldn't have been so worried if I'd been able to assure myself I really understood what Grandma was up to. In most ways, what she was forcing us to do *did* make sense. There were logical reasons why she might want to save some swamp water while she had the chance. She might want to increase her own powers. She also might want a stockpile just as insurance, in case it turned out that the effects faded with time.

It was also clear that Grandma could not physically negotiate the fence. She needed a young body for that, and here I was, conveniently yoked to a journal that was enough of a prod that she could use its exposure alone to force me to do what she wanted. I didn't even really blame her for blackmailing me, because I could see the logic of it. Without the journal she would have had to give me more than a cursory explanation in order to coerce me to carry out this errand; she might have had to give away her secret, and her wanting to keep the secret made a lot of sense.

But the one thing that did *not* make sense, and that made the whole business so confusing, was why she wanted Annelise to be involved. The question wouldn't stop gnawing at me. I could have gotten the water myself. Including Annelise was so irrational that it demolished the credibility of the rest of Grandma's motivation and gave the maneuver a nightmarish quality.

What was Grandma really up to anyway?

The plastic half gallon water jug, the ladle, and the rubber gloves and rain gear were hidden behind the shrubbery next to Grandma's house, as she had said they would be. I was quietly stuffing them into my backpack when I sensed Annelise's approach.

What I noticed first, before she even came in sight, was the fizzling sparkle of Annelise's delight at participating in this clandestine operation. But I could see beneath it now, down to Annelise's fury at me. All the attention I had paid to Lindie at lunch today still rankled. The fact that Eric had been fawning over her didn't make up for it. She wanted *everyone* to adore her.

I turned toward the sound of her footsteps as she strolled toward me. I could barely see her in the darkness, but I sensed that she was smiling, expertly hiding her hostile feelings. "This whole thing is crazy, but maybe it's kind of like an adventure," she said pleasantly.

"Uh . . . good way to look at it," I said, trying to sound equally pleasant.

Luckily she wasn't in a talkative mood. It began to drizzle when we were halfway there, not having spoken another word to each other. I pulled off the backpack, silently handed Annelise one of the rain-proof ponchos, and put the other one on myself. We plodded along the wet road, over the crest of the hill, and started down the incline. It was so dark with no moonlight that I could see only blackness at the bottom of the hill, though I knew the swamp and the fence around it were directly ahead of us now.

Better weather would have been nice. The flashlight would help us see—at the risk of attracting attention—but it would not make the grass around the swamp less slippery.

What I wanted was to collect the swamp water myself, leaving Annelise safely outside the fence, keeping watch. But I was sure she'd reject anything I suggested. I had to be clever and try to manipulate her into coming up with this plan on her own.

"So, uh, you have any ideas about how we should go about this?" I asked her.

"Just wait until we get there and see what the situation is," she said.

Grandma had absolutely forbidden us to check out the fence during the day. She was afraid that if we exhibited any curiosity, the place might be more heavily secured. We had to play it by ear, in the darkness and rain.

"But once we get there, we'll have to move fast," I said. "If we have plan A and plan B, we won't have to waste time down there deciding. Like, for instance, what we do if there's a gate we can get through or what we do if the gate's locked."

"If it's open, we go through; if it's locked, we climb over."

"Well, if we have to climb over, you think we should both go?" I dared say. "Or maybe one of us should stay outside to keep watch?"

She glanced at me now; I could just see the glint of her teeth as she smiled. She spoke softly above the hiss of the rain, though what she really wanted was to scream at me. "Thanks for wanting to protect me, Jared; I appreciate it. But I don't know what you're so afraid is going to happen to me. It's only fair if we both do our part. OK? One person holds the flashlight; the other one fills the jug. We both climb the fence." She looked hard at me and turned away again.

I stifled my sigh. But I couldn't stifle the tension that danced painfully through my muscles, so much worse than the feeling just before a race because now there was so much more that could go wrong. The curiosity Annelise felt was stronger than it had been this afternoon, and the suggestion I had just made only increased it. Annelise was more determined than ever to get as close as I did to the swamp. The stench, more pungent with every step, did not seem to bother her.

Now the tracery of a cyclone fence swam ghostlike in the darkness only a few yards ahead. It grew more solid, damp and vaguely glistening, as we approached. We stepped off the road onto wet grass sloping toward it.

I slipped and skidded, slamming into a post, grabbing wildly at the fence to keep from losing my balance. The metal web quivered against my cold fingers, my pulse as unsteady as my feet. It would be worse on the other side, where the slope was steeper. I disengaged one hand to wipe the water out of my eyes, warm water as well as cool, sweat and rain combined.

"You OK, Jared?" Annelise murmured from the left, scornful and superior, already feeling her way along to find the gate. She was thinking that Bruce would have been a lot more adept at this than I was. And she was itching to get over the fence.

I moved along the fence to the right, in case the gate might be that way. In a moment my hand slipped through a gap about an inch wide; an instant later my fingers closed around the padlock. "It's over here," I whispered, feeling only slightly less like a fool. I shook the gate gently, though I already knew it was locked.

"Locked, huh? So we climb," Annelise said, already beside me. And then she was energetically hoisting herself up, the fence vibrating again as she found footholds in the webbing. She saw no danger here. She was not afraid. She was only curious—and angry at me.

I quickly clambered up, my hands reaching for the top, desperate to get to the other side before she did. Whoever got there first would be more likely to fall in, and if anybody was going to fall in, it had to be me. Once Annelise actually saw it happen and realized how disgusting it was, she'd probably be a lot more careful.

At least there was no barbed wire, but the metal was slick, my grip insecure. I hung on, panting. I stretched my right foot up over the top, shifted my body, then jammed one toe through the mesh on the other side. Getting my behind over was the most awkward part. I had to keep moving my hands along the bar to find a position that would work, and several times my greasy palms slipped alarmingly and I almost fell.

Annelise was having an easier time. She was lighter, more agile, her smaller feet more secure in the mesh. She was over the top; she was on the way down. And then I sensed that she was about to let go and simply drop down onto the ground.

"Don't jump!" I gasped. "It's steeper on this side. You'll fall in."

Her head snapped toward me. "What makes you think I was going to jump? How do you know it's steeper over here?"

"I—I just thought that's what you would do. And I ride past here on my bike all the time."

"Thanks for the helpful advice," she said, very

suspicious of me now for knowing more than I should have. But she didn't jump; we both eased ourselves carefully down to the ground.

The reek of the water was so thick now I could feel it like slime on my skin. And the slope on this side was even steeper than I had realized. Clinging to the fence with one hand, then the other, I slipped off my pack. Then I squatted carefully down, my back propped against the fence, and reached into the pack, feeling around, pushing things aside, not finding what I wanted.

"Just give me the jug. Hurry," Annelise said.

I ignored her. There was no way I was going to give her the jug. Filling it would be my job. Annelise would hold the light. I had reached Grandma's house first; I was carrying the stuff. At least I had that much control. Finally my hand closed around the corrugated plastic flashlight. I thrust it at her, and one pair of gloves.

It was so dark that she didn't even know what I had given her until her fingers closed around it. She instantly pushed it back at me. "Give me the jug, Jared," she said.

But I was already inching away from her. I put on one glove, then the other. I pulled out the jug and the ladle. I set the pack down and moved toward the water on my hands and knees, not daring to stand up. "If you want to help, just turn on the light. I can't see a thing," I hissed at her.

She didn't turn on the flashlight; she jammed it roughly into my shoulder. "Oh, sorry," she said, as though it had been an accident. "Let me do my part, too, Jared." And then her other hand was on the jug, grappling for it.

I hadn't expected it to be as bad as this, that we would actually be tussling on the edge. I couldn't push her away; she might fall in. I hugged the jug to my chest. "Please, Annelise!" I begged her. "I know this place better than you. Just turn on the light so we can get it over with."

"Why do you know this place better than I do? What haven't you told me?" she demanded, struggling to get the jug away from me. "You're hiding something. What is it?"

I wrenched the jug away from her and crawled toward the water, refusing to answer her. If she wouldn't turn on the light, I'd feel my way. I'd touched the water already; it wouldn't matter if I got a little more on me now. I reached the edge. I stretched out the ladle and felt it enter the water.

"Tell me what you're hiding," Annelise said, panting, kneeling beside me, barely hiding her rage at me. She was gripping the jug again now, still trying to get it away from me, the unlit flashlight in her other hand. But I was stronger than she was. I emptied the ladle into the jug, dipped out more water, and dumped water into the jug again, then again.

"Let go of the jug, Annelise," I said, my voice choking in my throat. "Grandma might not give you your journal if she found out you made it so hard for me to get this stuff."

"You tell her that, and you won't *believe* what I'll

tell her about you!" she threatened, her voice rising harshly.

I went cold all over. What terrified me wasn't her threat but the inside of her mind. It was more foul than the swamp, like a swarm of flies in a wild food frenzy around rotten meat again, dizzying me. She was furious that she wasn't getting her own way and that I might be hiding something from her. But what she really couldn't stand was that I obviously just didn't like her anymore. That was what almost drove her completely out of control, her hand shaking on the jug.

But I had finished. The jug was sloshing over. Maybe it was going to be OK. "You can lay off, Annelise; I've got enough now," I said, starting to turn away from the water. And I couldn't resist adding, "And because I'm a nice guy, I won't tell Grandma how hard you made it."

And then she *did* go out of control. She made a savage snarling sound, jumped to her feet, and kicked out at me so violently that she lost her balance and fell backward into the swamp.

eleven

I was still in a state of shock when we reached Grandma's house.

It was bad enough that the water had touched Annelise at all. But the grass had been so slick in the darkness, giving neither of us any firm footing, that she kept sliding back in. Annelise had been exposed to the water for several minutes at least—maybe even longer than Grandma.

At her hysterical insistence I was numbly carrying the foul poncho she had been wearing, as well as the heavy water jug. But it was only a partial relief when I was finally able to shove the poncho behind the shrubbery; the stench still clung to Annelise's wet hair and clothes.

As upset as she was, Annelise was still thinking. "Don't bring the jug inside!" she hissed, and I set it down just off the stoop.

The side door opened as we stepped up to it, and Grandma silently ushered us into the dimly lit kitchen, a cigarette hanging from her mouth. No one said a word until the door was locked behind us.

"My God!" Grandma rasped, clasping her hands in dismay. "That smell! Annelise. Don't tell me. Oh, you poor child! You—you fell *in?*"

Annelise had regained her usual facade of sweetness. She nodded slowly. "I—I don't understand," she said, no rancor in her voice, only wounded virtue. "I kept trying to do my part. But Jared wouldn't let me help. He kept pulling the jug away from me. That's . . . why I fell in."

Grandma dropped the cigarette into an overflowing ashtray and turned to me, confusion on her face. "But why, Jared? Why?"

An instant later she was reaching for a large roll of heavy-duty aluminum foil, obviously placed there on the kitchen table for our return. She knelt and spread a couple of sheets on the floor for Annelise to drip on. Foil would not absorb the stuff the way newspaper would; she could save the drippings. She had expected Annelise to fall in! She had planned on it all along. She was prepared.

And suddenly all the acting going on around me was just too much. How could the truth do any damage now? *You know why, Grandma,* I silently answered her, concentrating the message into a pencil-thin laser beam focused directly into her brain. *I was getting the water myself to try to keep her from falling in. The last thing in the world I wanted was for her to be like us. But you arranged for her to be there, right on the edge. You wanted it to happen this way.* I shook my head. *You can go on denying it forever. It won't change what I know.*

Come on in again, Jared. Grandma welcomed me, with no inkling of surprise.

I hadn't been able to hide my powers from her after all. She already knew I was a reader! She pounced into my brain as I tumbled into hers, expecting the cottage in the woods, the cozy firelit room. . . .

The air throbbed with ratcheting and clacketing, hammering at the eardrums. Grandma and I were sitting on horsehair couches on a jittery cast-iron platform, suspended above an endless expanse of busy old-fashioned knitting machinery. Large spiders ran along catwalks below us, never stopping to rest, their jointed arms darting in and out among whirling bobbins and plunging needles.

Huh? Where are we?

What's the surprise? You've been here before, Jared. Grandma had the open photograph album in her lap. She looked down at it, then back to me. She smiled. *Remember this?*

"What is the matter with you two?" I could barely hear Annelise complaining under the sound of the machines, but I could still sense her irritation at being suddenly ignored for a few seconds instead of fussed over and comforted.

Yeah, but . . . your brain wasn't anything like this before.

You've got a lot to learn, Jared. I see you have a rudimentary idea of shields. But you haven't even begun to understand what you can really do with them.

It was beginning to sink in. *You mean . . . that cottage I saw before was fake? It was just a trap?* The cottage *had* been uncharacteristically neat and tidy, I now realized. Was this relentlessly productive factory closer to what Grandma's mind was *really* like?

Grandma only smiled and closed the album and set it aside.

"Why isn't anybody saying anything?" Annelise whined.

OK, OK, I'll try to figure that part out later, I told her, wiping sweat from my forehead. *But right now what I want to know is . . . why did you make Annelise go to the swamp with me? Why did you want her to fall in?*

That's for me to know and you to find out, dear, Grandma shot back at me. I felt her self-satisfaction like a heavy woolen jacket on a sweltering summer day.

I moved suddenly to look deeper, lunging for the answer to my question—and found myself hanging from the edge of the balcony, my feet inches above the eager, hungry machinery. The factory, or shield, or whatever it was, was impenetrable. I hoisted myself up, grunting, and flopped onto the couch, exhausted. *But you know what she's really like*, I gasped. *I felt it in you, you actually said it in words this afternoon—utterly amoral, chilling, a sociopath. And then you went and gave her this power. You created a monster! Er . . . sorry for the cliché. It just popped out.*

Apology accepted. The cliché is apt.

Then why?

I have the right to some secrets, even from you, my dear.

"Grandma, why are you just ignoring me?" Annelise whimpered.

Grandma and I turned toward her and jumped in. Not being a reader yet, Annelise's mind was dim, like a half-lit telephone booth with a crackling speaker-phone. But we could tell she was simmering with indignation at not being the center of attention for a few seconds. And she was more curious than ever, aware that something very peculiar was going on between Grandma and me that she was left out of.

She was as yet unaware of any change in herself. I thought back, remembering that I hadn't noticed anything until at least an hour after contact with the water. I had been too upset to think of looking at my watch when Annelise fell in, but I estimated that she still had more than half an hour before the first sensations would begin. It would be some time after that before she would realize what the sensations meant.

And if Grandma and I both set up barriers, Annelise might not be aware of any sensations at all until she woke up tomorrow.

Right on, Jared, coming up with the appropriate strategy on your own.

The thought was beamed at me even while Grandma was saying aloud, "I don't intend to be rude, darling, but do you have any idea what you smell like? You can hardly blame us for cringing and trying not to breathe a whole lot. Really, you ought to be grateful I even let you in the house. To the shower with you, this moment. Jared, make a path of foil for her."

"I'm sorry, Grandma. Of course I'm grateful. But that wasn't what I meant. Uh . . ." Annelise's shy hesitancy would have convinced anyone but Grandma and me. "I just meant . . . aren't you forgetting something?"

"Forgetting something?" Grandma said, sounding genuinely puzzled. Of course, she knew exactly what Annelise was referring to; she was just enjoying the sweet, sadistic kick of playing with her this way. "Room deodorizer, is that what you mean? I'll get to that as soon as you're out of the kitchen. Or maybe it's baby oil you want. There's vats of it in the bathroom, dear, I assure you."

It was all Annelise could do not to stamp her foot, but she merely shot me a glance and then smiled at Grandma. "We have what you wanted us to get, Grandma. Right, Jared?"

"Right," I agreed with her.

"So . . . didn't you promise to give us something in return?" Annelise hit me with another look.

"We have the jug, Grandma. It's full," I said, knowing Annelise was expecting me to back her up. And of course I wanted my journal, too.

"Oh, I see, you're still concerned about your little notebooks," Grandma said, as though they were completely irrelevant. She reached out her hand, wiggling her fingers. "Jared will give me the jug now, and I'll give the notebooks to him while you're in the shower, Annelise. You certainly wouldn't want to touch yours with that gunk all over your hands."

"Thanks for your concern, Grandma. But I won't mind if it gets a little dirty." Annelise, who didn't realize I already knew the contents of much of her journal, had no intention of letting me get my hands on it even for an instant. She was furious at Grandma and also frightened. But she didn't want to argue with Grandma or demand the notebooks first herself. She turned to me for help. She wanted *me* to come across as the tough one.

"We'd like to have the notebooks first, Grandma," I said. *Don't tell me you're going to try to hold out on us.*

Of course not. I just love making her squirm.

Well, I suggest you stop playing around and let us have the notebooks now. The sooner she gets cleaned up and goes to sleep, the less likely she'll be to notice anything until tomorrow. And the more time we have before she knows what she can do, the more time we'll have to plan some kind of defense. OK?

"What if I want the water first?" Grandma said aloud.

"Don't bother trying," I told her. "You don't give us the notebooks, we dump out the stuff, and you'll never get it."

"You wouldn't dare," Grandma said.

"It'll just take me a second to kick the jug over." I turned and reached for the door.

"No! Wait. Stop!" Grandma cried.

I turned back and said quietly, "Please get the notebooks."

Grandma saluted me. "Yes, sir. Right away, sir," she briskly replied, and marched from the room.

"Jeez, I didn't know you had it in you," Annelise whispered. She was surprised by my unexpected assertiveness with Grandma. She would have expected it of Bruce, but not pathetic Jared.

"There's a lot you don't know about me," I said, and that was true at the moment.

But it wouldn't be for long.

twelve

While Annelise showered, Grandma gave me some pointers on elementary-level shield construction. I didn't have the skill yet to manufacture entire environments, like Grandma's cottage and factory. All I could manage for now was something similar to wall-papering an old room, pasting up a bland cosmetic surface to hide what was underneath.

Annelise was in the bathroom for twenty-five minutes, but she still seemed to be noticing nothing when she finally emerged. I left with Annelise, both of us clutching our notebooks. The outer surface of my shield was the contents of my journal. Underneath that I could maintain nothing more complicated than a solid wall of ice, and even the ice was rather loosely and unevenly in place, the journal peeling off and slipping around the edges. Annelise kept asking me why Grandma wanted the swamp water. I'm not sure how convincingly ignorant I came across. But luckily she was just too tired to devote much energy to grilling me about it. As soon as Annelise was safely inside her cottage, I sneaked back to Grandma's. The two of us stayed up until dawn.

I wasted a lot of time continuing to ask Grandma why she had given Annelise the power. I took every opportunity I could find to try to slip inside and find out the answer myself. Her factory shield remained impermeable and deafening. All she would allow me to see of her motivation was *I had no choice.*

I tried to reason directly with her. *I'm not hiding anything from you. You already know I don't exactly approve of the other things you did—robbing the bank, blackmailing the Winstons to sell their house—but at least I can understand why. But Annelise! It's worse than senseless; it's worse than suicidal. It's like giving Hitler the atomic bomb.*

You don't find the situation invigorating, entertaining?

Yeah, entertaining like being locked up with a serial killer.

If you don't calm down, you're going to turn out to be a drawback rather than an asset.

I changed my tack. *Why do you want the swamp water?*

She put down her knitting and lit another cigarette, sharing nothing with me but the nicotine rush, which was deeply pleasurable to her but made me feel sick. I darted away from it.

"Good," she said out loud, and blew out smoke. "Now maybe you'll stop pestering me and try to help."

"OK. So what kind of strategy do you have in mind?" I asked her. "We don't have much time. She's not dumb. It'll only take her a couple of hours to figure out what she can do."

She tapped her cigarette in the ashtray, staring down at it, her mouth tensing as though she were trying not to smile. "Surprise me, Jared. You tell me."

I sighed in frustration. "But you must have had something in mind, or else you never would have done this to her. Why won't you tell me *anything?*"

"I want you to figure it out for yourself. I need proof of your usefulness to me. If I don't get it, I'll operate on my own."

I was beginning to understand why her children felt the way they did about her. Superficially she came across as wryly wacky and eccentric, even refreshing in an acid sort of way. But underneath she was as stubborn as a bank vault, as inexorable as a wrecking ball when it came to having her own way. She was powerful; I wanted her on my side. But she wasn't making it easy.

"OK," I said. "Let's say we manage to keep our shields in place. She'll still figure a lot of things out pretty fast, once she begins to realize she's reading. She knows you fell in the swamp, then you knew where our journals were hidden and you wanted more swamp water. She'll put two and two together. Shield or not, she'll know you're a reader. She'll know it before the day is over. There's no way to prevent it."

Watching me through her glasses, Grandma nodded.

"And then she'll know what you did: the ATM, the repairs to the house, breaking into the Winstons' and blackmailing them. You know from her journal how she uses information about people. It'll be her weapon, her way of making you powerless to stop her, and also her way of getting anything else she wants from you."

Grandma's face hardened, though I wasn't telling her anything she didn't know already. "Go on," she murmured, lighting another cigarette.

"But . . . I don't think there's any evidence pointing at me, if I can keep up my shield. Annelise doesn't know I fell in the swamp. I was as surprised as she was about the journal; you used it to blackmail me, too. She won't automatically know I'm a reader—especially if you make it clear to her that

I'm as ordinary and ignorant as everybody else. You'll go along with that, right?"

"Maybe. If you can prove to me why I should."

The reason why seemed obvious. But Grandma wasn't going to give me a crumb until I had earned it to her satisfaction by spelling everything out. "OK," I said, clenching my fists on the table, stifling my impatience. "If she doesn't know I'm a reader, that'll be *our* secret weapon against her. She won't shield herself from me."

"Not too bad, Jared. You're finally beginning to get somewhere," Grandma admitted, staring meditatively at the burning end of her cigarette. "But Annelise is already a prodigy at manipulation. She'll learn how to attack us fast. There are so many opportunities right here in the family. Whoever either of us cares about, that's who she'll take as a hostage. . . ."

I tried not to think of Lindie; it was something I would need a lot of practice at. I didn't know whether Grandma knew Lindie's secret or not, but I didn't want her to find out about it from me. Grandma was an angel of mercy compared with Annelise, but she was plenty unscrupulous herself. I still didn't know how much I could trust her.

"I'm not saying we don't have to try to keep your power a secret from her. That will help. But it's not enough." Grandma shook her head. "The only real safety is prevention. Stopping her for good before she really gets started."

"You know more about this power than I do, Grandma. Can you use it to zap her? Disable her somehow, so she can't do any harm?"

Grandma put her hand to her throat, pretending to be shocked. "My own darling granddaughter?"

I wanted to scream. "But you said she had to be stopped! And if you believe she has to be stopped, then why did you make her go to the swamp in the first place?"

"Because I knew it was the only way to stop her."

For a moment I just stared at her in blank disbelief. Then I pounded my fists on the table; the spiderweb swayed. "What are you talking about? That's crazy! It doesn't make any sense at all!"

She watched me, unsmiling, offering no sympathy, no explanation. "If you can't figure it out for yourself, you'll never really understand. And if you don't really understand, you won't be an asset, you'll be a hindrance. And no, I can't *zap* people, as you so crudely put it—though it would certainly be a useful device to have at my disposal."

She sighed wistfully, then shook her head and became businesslike again. "No zapping. But Annelise *does* have a weakness we might be able to use, to get her to dig her own grave. Tell me where she is vulnerable, Jared. You tell me that, I let you in. You don't tell me, then I leave you out. You'll be on your own." She looked at her watch, letting the threat hang in the air like the smoke that filled the room.

"You—you don't really mean that, Grandma," I

said, knowing that she did. I thought of the uncrackable vault and the wrecking ball. And then I forced myself to concentrate hard on Annelise and the terrible things in her journal and in her mind.

And that, of course, was where the answer was.

thirteen

I paused briefly outside Grandma's kitchen door as the sun splashed the first daubs of pale paint across the dark water. I had seen a sunrise here once before, last year, imagining myself following the magic golden path over the waves. I ached now, remembering how simple and benign the world had once been.

I sneaked unnoticed into the cottage. Not even bothering to take off my clothes, I collapsed onto the bed and fell instantly asleep, exhaustion weightier than all my anxiety.

Everyone has experienced the relief of waking from a nightmare and gradually, joyously realizing that it was only a dream. Waking today was the reverse.

It was around noon when I began to emerge from painless oblivion into nagging tension, then vague dread, and finally the specifics of panic. Sunlight streamed through the window. The world only darkened and sprouted murderous claws and fangs as my awareness of the situation clarified.

What terrible things was Annelise going to do? And who would be her first victim?

I sat up and rubbed my eyes and looked around the room, trying to shake the nightmare feeling. And it increased, all the ordinary familiar objects turning malignant. "Color me ugly, color me cruel, color me out to get you," whispered the bright plastic alarm clock, the overflowing bookcase, the white curtain flapping gently in the breeze. Everything was tainted, everything a threat. I groaned and burrowed under the sheet and squeezed my eyes shut. But the monster was real, and there was no avoiding her.

And through whatever was going to happen I would have to maintain a convincing *inner* (as well as outer) countenance of placid ignorance and normality. I didn't see how I could possibly do it. But if I didn't do it, if I slipped for only a fraction of a second and Annelise caught me, there would never be any safety again. Even before she was a reader, Annelise had *already* had the ability to inflict terrible damage on anyone who interfered with her image or got in the way of what she wanted. She had gone so far as to cause someone's death in a boating accident. And now that she had this special power, what she'd be able—and eager—to do was beyond imagining.

Mom and Dad were gone. I had no appetite, but I put together my peanut butter, salami, and cheese sandwich and forced it all down, hoping that going through the motions, even unobserved, would give me practice in keeping up my act.

Then I had another idea. I went back upstairs and wrote in my journal a description of the last two days' events, leaving out falling in the swamp, leaving out my own ESP, writing it as though I knew only what I wanted Annelise to believe I knew. I did this not only in case Annelise might physically read the journal, though that was certainly a possibility, but mainly to have the actual words down there in the notebook and in my mind. The more current the journal was, the more convincing a shield it would make. Simply writing the entry down implanted it photographically in my brain; enhancing your memory seemed to be another effect of the swamp water. I also glanced at *Anna Karenina* on the bedside table. I could use that as more wallpaper over the ice.

And then, in swimsuit and flip-flops, a big red-and-white-striped beach towel draped over my shoulders, I walked to the beach, hoping Annelise wouldn't be there.

She was down by the water, playing with Amy

again. But Annelise was not bored by Amy today; she watched the small child with an unusually intent, alert expression, often whispering to her. A good place to begin, a simpler mind to explore first, practicing, testing what she could do, before moving on to more complex prey.

Such as blackmailing Grandma about the ATM and the Winstons. And also Lindie. I hadn't looked deeply enough at what Lindie had done to find out exactly how to expose her, since it had never occurred to me to do it. Annelise wouldn't hesitate. I knew from her journal how eager she was to lash out at Lindie.

Concentrating on *Anna Karenina*, I greeted Mom and Dad and Aunt Maggie and Uncle Eric, making a conscious effort not to read them. Annelise would soon be dipping into my mind. If she detected anyone else's thoughts in there, she'd know I was a reader. Then she'd hide her thoughts from me, and Grandma and I would have no way of surprising her.

I sat down on my towel, looking toward the ocean. Eric was waist-deep in the water, plodding toward the shore, his eyes fixed on Annelise. He'd be a good one for her to feed on next. His blind adoration of her would be more delectable than fried clams and not the least bit fattening.

Lindie was still swimming. How was I going to keep Lindie and her secret away from Annelise without making Annelise suspicious?

And at that moment the world grew even more menacing. The sun was the unblinking eye of a colossal cyclops, the ocean a gigantic amoebalike organism of digestion. Because it hit me with full force what hiding my power from Annelise really meant: It meant I couldn't read Annelise either.

Last night I had thought that if I kept my powers hidden from Annelise, she wouldn't shield herself from me. Then I could sneak into her mind, find out what she was planning to do, and alert Grandma in time to stop her. I had believed that was our secret weapon.

But now I knew it wouldn't work. Because Annelise, like Grandma, had been in the swamp longer than I had. If I peeked into Annelise's mind, she'd know it—just as Grandma had known when I'd thought I was secretly probing *her* mind. And as soon as Annelise knew I was a reader, she'd shield her mind from me and use her power against me in any destructive way she could. So I couldn't read Annelise, I couldn't read anybody else, I could only hide my powers completely. Grandma and I had no secret weapon after all.

We also had no real plan, only a sort of vague idea based on Annelise's one weakness. Exactly what we did would have to depend on what Annelise's first move was. And now that I knew I couldn't read her, we'd have no advance warning.

So why hadn't Grandma pointed that out to me last night? Why was she still hiding things from me? How much could I really trust her?

Annelise was standing up, facing the water, talking and laughing with Eric now, who was facing away from the sea. And Lindie was heading toward them, finishing her swim. I had to keep Lindie away from Annelise.

I pushed myself up from the towel and moved toward the water, forcing myself to walk slowly, to appear casual, when what I really wanted was to run, yelling and waving my hands. I reminded myself that it would be awhile before Annelise had the power and the skill to penetrate Lindie's shell. But I still didn't want her to know that the shell even existed. Lindie was one of her special targets. As soon as she knew there was something hidden and useful there, she would pursue it relentlessly.

I drew nearer to Annelise and Eric as Lindie approached the shore. I concentrated on my journal; I thickened the ice beneath it. *Neither of us could figure out why Grandma wanted that stuff or how she ever found our journals. . . .*

Annelise smiled at me—enough to give Eric a jealous twinge. "You look like you just got up, Jared," she said. "You must have been up really late last night."

"Yeah, I, uh, didn't get to sleep until pretty late," I said, thinking of Kitty and Levin, Anna and Vronsky—and forcing myself *not* to wonder what Annelise was seeing in my mind.

"Oh, come off it, Jared," Annelise pleasantly teased me. "I can always tell when you're hiding something. If you went to some great party without telling us, we'll really be mad. Won't we, Eric?"

"Maybe he was just reading," Eric shyly defended me.

"Or was it that girl over on Indian Neck?" Annelise went on as Lindie reached us. I could have punched her for that. Of course, Annelise knew where I had been last night—or thought she did. She was enjoying putting me on the spot, knowing my problem with lying. Did she also know enough to start trying to create a rift between Lindie and me?

I didn't even have to look into Lindie's mind to know she was aware that Annelise was playing some kind of game. It was the way she watched Annelise without expression. Her astuteness about Annelise only made me feel closer to her. I also noticed the glow of her skin after her swim. And was it only my imagination, or did her bathing suit actually seem a little too big for her now?

"Uh, Lindie. There's something I wanted to ask you, about Tolstoy." I beckoned her away from the others. That was what Annelise would expect me to do as a way of worming out of the uncomfortable situation she had put me in.

"Yeah?" Lindie said, toweling off, striding along beside me, as eager to get away from Annelise and her games as I was. But she wasn't smiling at me as she had yesterday. Was she wondering if I really *did* know a girl on Indian Neck? I was still too close to Annelise to read Lindie and find out.

"Levin is really Tolstoy, right?" I said as we moved farther away from Annelise and Eric.

"Everybody knows that," Lindie said, shrugging.

"Was Kitty supposed to be Tolstoy's wife, then?"

"I never really thought about that," Lindie said. "I kind of doubt it, though. I mean—"

"Amy!" Annelise shrieked.

I was so startled in the instant it took us to spin around that I briefly dropped my shield and was suddenly blasted by Annelise's mind. She was crowing with elation at her first successful gambit. She had distracted me, Eric, and Lindie on purpose, so that we would not be thinking about Amy. She had also checked on everyone else, making sure they all assumed that someone else was keeping an eye on Amy and were not watching her themselves.

And then Annelise had allowed Amy to run straight into the water. And keep on going.

She had been watching her, fully aware of what Amy was doing. She had done nothing to stop her. She had waited until this moment to act. And at this moment Amy was nowhere to be seen. She had gone under.

Fast as Lindie was, it was Annelise, knowing Amy's exact location, who got to her first. It was Annelise who pulled Amy out, Annelise who carried her limp body to shore, Annelise who knelt over her and skillfully began mouth-to-mouth resuscitation.

We all were standing around them, Aunt Grace clinging hysterically to Uncle Ted. Nobody said a word. I had put my shield back, but I knew that underneath their worries about Amy, everyone was thinking: Who was supposed to be watching her?

Annelise breathed into Amy's mouth; she turned

her head and spit out a little water; she breathed into her mouth again. I knew from her journal that she had learned mouth-to-mouth resuscitation in school. She was coolly businesslike about the whole thing, as anyone trying to save a life should be.

"Please, please," Aunt Grace sobbed.

Amy stirred. She coughed. Her eyes fluttered open. She seemed confused for only a moment. Very quickly she grinned and opened her arms to Annelise.

Annelise hugged her back warmly; she pressed her cheek against Amy's for a long moment, whispering to her. Then she modestly stepped away and allowed Aunt Grace to swoop Amy into her arms.

"Are you OK, sweetheart? You feel OK?"

"I went swimming!" Amy cried gleefully.

"You're really OK?"

"Sure. What's the matter? Why are you crying, Mommy?"

"Amy, you must never, never go near the water by yourself again!" Aunt Grace said sternly, shaking her just a little. "Do you know that you almost died? If it weren't for Annelise . . ."

The release of everyone's tension was palpable in the silence that followed. Then suddenly they were hugging Annelise, heaping her with praise. She loved it. She kept shaking her head, acting embarrassed, saying it was nothing. And then she turned to Eric.

"Eric," Annelise said, sounding frightened, "I told you to keep an eye on her."

"You—you did?" Eric was utterly confused.

Annelise's strategy was ingenious. Eric was so besotted, and saw Annelise as so virtuous, that it would never occur to him that she might blame him for something that was really her fault. It was much easier for him to believe that she really *had* asked him to keep his eye on Amy and that he had forgotten. In Annelise's presence he usually did forget everything but her.

"Oh, I'm so sorry!" he desperately apologized, actually wringing his hands in guilt and despair. And that was all it took to establish that what had happened to Amy really had been Eric's fault.

"Thank heaven you were so alert, Annelise," gushed Aunt Grace, cradling Amy again, not looking at Eric. She was probably too furious to allow herself to speak to him.

Most of the others were still heaping praise on Annelise, and I knew that Annelise was hungrily lapping it up. The exceptions were Aunt Maggie, who was glaring at Eric, and Lindie and I, who were saying nothing. If things had been different, I could have defended Eric. I could have told them that Annelise had said nothing about Amy to him. But I couldn't say that. It would have attracted Annelise's suspicion. There was nothing I could do to help him.

I could only watch Annelise, her expression radiating deep concern for Amy, while at the same time I struggled to think about my journal, backed up by a ten-mile-thick barrier of ice. Even now, with more practice, I couldn't come up with anything more elaborate than that; like lying, complex shield construction seemed to be a talent I just didn't have.

Was the ice enough to prevent Annelise from knowing I was a reader? In only a few hours of awareness she had already won the first round.

And then she stumbled slightly; her mouth dropped open. Something had clearly socked her with unexpected force.

In the next moment Grandma, who had just appeared beside me, spoke. "What was the matter with you, Annelise?" she said quietly.

Everyone turned toward Grandma. "Uh . . . matter?" Annelise said, barely managing to utter even that much. She must have known what Grandma was about to say.

"Was it some kind of fit, a trance or something?" Grandma asked her. "I saw it in my telescope. You were staring directly at Amy, watching her run out into the water, and doing nothing to stop her."

The family turned back to Annelise now, shock on their faces. Surprised as she was, she quickly pulled herself together, putting on a puzzled expression. "I guess you don't understand, Grandma," she said earnestly. "I asked Eric to keep an eye on her. He promised he would."

"Do you really believe that, Annelise?" Grandma asked her, sounding worried. "You know I've been reading lips with my telescope for decades. Whatever you may imagine, you said *nothing* to Eric about watching Amy. Did she, Eric?"

Everyone had plenty of proof that Grandma could read lips; she never tired of bragging about it, giving specific examples. And Eric was not enough of a fool, despite the way he felt about Annelise, to go on accepting the terrible blame when he now had solid evidence of what Annelise had done to him—not to mention to Amy. "Uh . . . no," he said miserably, looking down at the sand, unable to face Annelise.

"Not only that, Annelise, dear," Grandma said. "I haven't forgotten what you were telling me the other day about lifesaving class. How it was so boring to practice it on that stupid Resussa-Annie doll instead of on a real person."

"Annelise told me about Resussa-Annie, too!" chirped Amy.

The rest of our family didn't speak. But their expressions, as they avoided looking at Annelise, were not pleasant at all.

Annelise's eyes flashed at Grandma. The war was on. And *we* had won the first battle after all.

fourteen

"Come, Annelise. We need to have a chat," Grandma said gently. "Maybe I can help. You look tired and stressed out, like you didn't get enough sleep last night. Maybe that's why you were so forgetful just now."

Annelise couldn't even allow herself to glare at Grandma. I could imagine how frustrated she must feel. There was nothing she could say—either to defend herself or to discredit Grandma—that would not make her look even worse.

"Come, dear," Grandma urged her.

And, meek on the surface, Annelise went.

Even though I couldn't let myself read Annelise, I was pretty sure she dreaded being alone with Grandma, not yet prepared for this confrontation with another reader. But to Annelise, anything would be preferable to the mystified, hostile feelings she must be getting from the family. They were beginning to think she might not be perfect! To Annelise, that would be like walking on burning coals, something intolerably painful that she had no choice but to escape from.

The others said nothing more about the incident. They would reserve their real feelings—as always—for the privacy of their cottages.

Lindie and I, in silent mutual agreement, strolled away from them again. We (Grandma, actually) had won the first round, and I was able to relax a little, since Annelise and Grandma were busy and out of range now. I let down my ice shield.

"Tired and stressed out?" Lindie scoffed, rolling her eyes. "Yeah, she's got a problem, all right, but it's a lot worse than that." Then she pressed her lips together and looked straight ahead, leaving her accusation implicit. Straightforward as she was, she was still hesitant to express all her very powerful negative feelings about Annelise to me. She wasn't into turning people against one another. If it hadn't been for her concern about Amy, she probably would have said even less.

"That's for sure. I bet Annelise knew exactly what

she was doing," I said. "She wanted everyone to think she was a heroine. She didn't care about Amy. But Grandma saw through her."

"So why does Grandma come up with this stress excuse?" Lindie asked me. "Grandma was the one who caught Annelise. And then right away she gives her an out. I don't get it."

"Grandma's, uh . . . complicated," I said. Lindie was smarter about people than I was. I was duped by Annelise until I read her mind; Lindie needed no special power to see through her. Now I wanted to prove to Lindie that I was insightful, too. I remembered what Grandma had said last night about letting Annelise dig her own grave. "Well, I think Grandma thought it was enough that she helped us all see for ourselves what Annelise did. Nobody really bought the stress excuse anyway. Also, Grandma wanted to come across as being fair to Annelise. If people thought Grandma was out to get her, then that *would* give Annelise an out—and weaken the real ammunition Grandma has against her."

Lindie was thinking I was smarter than she had realized, and that bolstered me a lot. "You're making it sound like it's a war," she said. "Is there something going on that I don't know about?"

I just couldn't resist continuing to impress Lindie. And I felt more confident now. "Well, from the changes I've noticed around here this year, I think Grandma might see life as a kind of war. Like a cold war, I mean. Like with spies, strategy, secret documents . . . maybe even blackmail," I hinted.

Lindie pondered this for a moment. Then she laughed. "You just gave me the craziest idea, Jared," she said, shaking her head at the absurdity of it. "Everybody knows Grandma's always hated the Winstons and wanted that property. Then the Winstons suddenly had to sell." She laughed briefly again, but her smile faded. "And the Winstons refused to say what was taken from their house, some secret thing. And Grandma and her telescope. The ATM robberies and all the improvements on Grandma's house." She gave me a funny look. Then she dropped her voice, even though there was no one else around. "Is that what you mean by a kind of war?"

"Well . . ."

"Jared, you can't seriously believe *Grandma* did those things!"

Lindie was even quicker than I had expected. "No, no," I said hastily. "All I meant was . . . well, you know what she's like. She might *imagine* doing them."

Lindie didn't answer, thinking hard.

We had wandered past the jetty now, to where the rocks began, and the only way to keep walking was to go up from the beach toward Grandma's house. I tried to squelch my intense curiosity about what was going on inside.

But did I really have to squelch it? I was sure Grandma and Annelise would be so preoccupied with each other that they wouldn't notice a little delicate hidden probing from me. My range was farther today; I was probably close enough now to get a whiff. I wasn't stupid enough to touch Annelise. And why should Grandma mind if I took a peek at her? I promised myself I would stick very close to the surface. I dipped a single toe into Grandma's mind, so slowly and cautiously I was sure it wouldn't cause even a ripple.

And wrenched it out of boiling oil, mentally howling in agony. What on earth was going on in there? I had never experienced anything like it.

"What's the matter, Jared?" Lindie said, reaching out to me. "Are you OK?"

I stared back at her concerned, innocent face. I had no idea what was going on inside the house, only that it was more brutal and powerful than anything I had felt before. And I was struck, too late, by what I had just done to Lindie.

I had told her too much. Because of what I had said, she had guessed about Grandma's crimes. Maybe she didn't really believe Grandma had done those things, but the thought was there, and that was enough. She was at risk from both Annelise and Grandma now.

But I had done even more than that. By peering so deeply into her own mind, I had weakened and cracked her protective shell, creating a channel that led directly to her secret, making it a lot easier for another reader to find.

If only I hadn't so stupidly tried to impress her! But it was too late to change it now. All I could do was try to protect her. "Let's go back to the beach,"

I urged her, anxious to escape from here in a hurry. Grandma's house had become the witch's cottage in "Hansel and Gretel." "I'm hot. I'm dying for a swim. Come on."

We started for the beach. A moment later the door slammed. I didn't want to turn back, but Lindie stopped, and I had to.

Grandma and Annelise stood next to each other just outside the kitchen doorway. Grandma, her white hair streaming down her back, wore the usual long printed skirt and big peasanty blouse that only emphasized the scrawniness of her arms, neck, and face. Dark-haired Annelise was as fresh and appetizing as a ripe peach, her lovely body encased in her gleaming salmon swimsuit. They both were staring hard at Lindie and me, reading us.

I was unprepared, fumbling. It took me almost an entire second to get my journal and the ten miles of ice in place. And during that second I was hit by two things: Annelise's glee and Grandma's bitter disappointment that I had given her secret away to Lindie.

We hadn't won the first round after all; I could feel that Annelise was no longer under Grandma's control. And I had betrayed Grandma. Would she ever forgive me or see me as an ally again? What was going to happen to Lindie now? We were in a worse mess than ever, and a lot of it was my fault. I jumped behind the shield, shakily planting my feet on the ice.

"You two must be dying of thirst. Come on in and have a cold drink," Grandma said, smiling around her cigarette.

"We're going swimming," I said quickly.

But Lindie had no idea what was really happening. And she was thirsty and curious. "Thanks, I'd love something to drink," she said. She stepped toward the door, then turned back. "Have a good swim, Jared."

"Uh . . . I guess I'll have something to drink after all," I said. I knew I was no match for Annelise or Grandma. But I couldn't leave Lindie alone with them.

fifteen

"Feeling better now, Annelise?" Lindie asked her with a trace of sarcasm as we stepped into the dark kitchen.

"Oh, I'm fine," Annelise said lightly, though her jaw was tense.

I resisted the dangerous urge to look inside her. At the same time I was having trouble with my shield; it was slippery for some reason.

But even though I couldn't read Annelise, I could tell by her manner that she was still somewhat unhinged by the battering of negative thoughts about her she had suffered on the beach. I was sure that her first objective would be to restore her benign image with the rest of the family. She would use anything she could find in anyone's mind to accomplish this. "How are *you* feeling, Lindie?" she asked sweetly.

"Uh, fine," Lindie said. She shot me a significant glance, to which I barely responded. Even with the shield, it was clear to me that Lindie naturally saw Annelise as the one who was in trouble, as she deserved to be, everyone in the family finally aware— as Lindie had always been—of how hateful she really was. And Annelise must know exactly what Lindie was thinking about her, and it would only madden her, and fan the burning coals, and make her more eager than ever to hurt Lindie somehow.

We sat down at the kitchen table. "Cola, Lindie?" Grandma asked her. "Iced tea? I know! How about a beer? You'll be drinking it at Harvard next year, if you haven't started already."

"Iced tea, no sugar, please," Lindie said, and turned back to Annelise. "What happened with Amy? Did you just kind of, you know, blank out or something?" she asked, while I struggled, inwardly gasping, to maintain my balance on my shield. It was definitely getting more slippery, as though the ice were melting. At the same time, I had no doubt Annelise, stimulated by the allure of treasure and revenge, was plowing relentlessly through Lindie's mind. Lindie's secret was less hidden than before, now that I had hacked away the foliage, trampled down the grass, laid the path that would lead directly toward it.

"I think we should talk about something else, Lindie, dear," Grandma said with warmth in her voice, handing Lindie what looked like very strong iced tea and thrusting a glass of beer at me.

"Er, thanks," I said. "But I really don't—"

"You'll love it. Drink it up," Grandma coolly ordered me. "There'll be more when you finish that one."

Lindie couldn't hide her surprise. "Excuse me, Grandma, but it's only two in the afternoon. And you're making Jared drink a beer he doesn't want?"

"It's OK. Maybe it's good," I said quickly, and took a hasty swallow. I had no choice; I couldn't disobey Grandma.

All I had sensed from Grandma outside was the sting of her disappointment in me for saying too much to Lindie. Since I was hiding my abilities from Annelise now, I couldn't read Grandma to find out any more. But I still had to hope that she might forgive me. And the only way I could think of to try to regain her confidence was to obey her every whim—meaning, drink the beer. I had to have Grandma on my side. Grandma was the only one who could possibly disarm Annelise. I had seen her do it on the beach today, and she might be able to do it again. And only with Grandma's help could I use the idea she had milked out of me about using Annelise's weakness against her.

Grandma had not made it easy for me last night.

She had refused to accept me as an ally until I came up on my own with Annelise's weak point.

I had already known that Annelise was desperate for the approval of others. But not until last night, under Grandma's pressure, had I seen Annelise's overwhelming need for admiration as a possible Achilles' heel. By the time it had finally dawned on me that this was her fatal flaw, it was too late to get into the specifics of exactly *how* we could use it to get her to dig her own grave. "Wait and see" was all Grandma had said. I had been too tired to think any further.

What had happened on the beach today had seemed to confirm what Grandma had said last night. Annelise had made a murderous bid to win even more approval; Grandma had turned it against her.

But Grandma had never spelled everything out, and I was beginning to doubt that she ever would. She was an enigma. And I was flying blind, completely dependent on her.

I didn't know what had happened between Grandma and Annelise when they were alone in the house, except for the gleeful flash I had gotten from Annelise that she was no longer under Grandma's control. Did that mean Grandma was under Annelise's control? They both were such good actors I couldn't tell, and I couldn't give myself away by reading them.

I finished the beer and set the glass down on the table. Grandma instantly replaced it with another one. I knew beer would impair my abilities. But I had no choice except to keep drinking, if that was what Grandma wanted.

"It's that good?" Lindie asked me curiously, finishing her iced tea.

"It's thirst-quenching," I told her, and that was the truth. It was dark and thick and bitter, though its taste was dulled by its icy coldness; Grandma must have had it in the freezer for a while.

My recalcitrant shield was giving me even more trouble now. There were visible cracks in the ice; I didn't seem to be able to keep them closed. What was melting it? It wasn't the beer; the shield had begun to weaken before I'd had a sip.

I felt a touch on my arm. "Maybe I *will* have a taste," Lindie said, smiling faintly at me.

I smiled back, handing her the glass. I was pretty sure Lindie was on my side. Lindie couldn't read, so she wouldn't be much help. But the way things were now, I couldn't read either. And a little beer might make us bolder, more forthright, tougher for a devious mind to understand and deal with. The more rash and uncalculating we were, the less predictable we'd be to Annelise. Maybe that was what Grandma intended.

"Gee, it actually tastes kind of good," Lindie said, surprised, as she passed the glass back to me.

"Go for it. There's more than enough for both of you," Grandma urged her, and before Lindie could refuse, she had set a full glass in front of her.

And Lindie drank it. She obligingly dropped the subject of Annelise's lapse. She answered their questions about going away to school next year. And she continued to smile at me.

I hadn't been paying much attention to Annelise; ignoring her made it easier to hide from her on the slick ice, though the cracks were widening. I was sliding around on an unsteady island. And now Annelise suddenly leaned forward, her eyes brightening. "It's almost impossible to get into Harvard, isn't it?" she said. "I mean, there's like ten times as many applicants as they can accept, or something like that, right?"

"I forget the exact figure," Lindie said, sounding bored, as though she wanted the subject to end there.

That encouraged Annelise. "I mean, they don't even consider you unless you have perfect SAT scores, right?" Annelise pressed her.

"Uh, yeah, the scores help," Lindie admitted, and took a quick gulp of beer, her discomfort showing. She must have allowed her secret to surface in her mind.

And I could tell that Annelise, leaning back in her chair, had caught it easily, with one hand.

"What's the matter, Lindie?" Grandma asked her. "You feeling OK?"

Lindie shook back her hair. She had remembered how she had cheated; it had stabbed at her consciousness; I had seen it on her face. But now she assumed a normal expression again and took another drink. "I'm fine," she said.

"Gee, Lindie, look at you swigging down that beer

in the middle of the day! You're turning out to be a lot cooler than I ever realized," Annelise said, beaming at her. "I know you better now."

"You think so?" Lindie said, staring hard at Annelise. "Funny it took you so long. *I* always knew *exactly* what you were like."

Annelise must be reading her deeply. She had already known Lindie didn't like her. But now Annelise was getting the full force of Lindie's resentment, her disapproval—and her disgust. I could tell Annelise didn't like it. She didn't like it at all. Even coming from someone as unimportant as Lindie, the burning coals might be almost enough to drive Annelise out of control again.

But not quite. Annelise gave a casual shrug. "You really aren't like I pictured you at all, Lindie. You fooled me. And you fooled the admissions people at Harvard, too. Don't you think they'd be surprised—and *fascinated*—to hear about Zippy?"

Grandma dropped her burning cigarette. Even though Lindie wasn't a reader, her shock wave had massive punch. I felt it, too, battering at my weakening shield, gaps widening as more pieces of ice cracked off and my rocking island shrank.

"Zippy . . . ," Lindie said expressionlessly as she gulped down a lot of beer, not knowing what else to do. It must have seemed to her that she had fallen into a nightmare, having no idea how Annelise had found out this information. "You—you know about him?" she asked.

"I know you bought the math SAT from him,"

Annelise said. "And I can prove it to Harvard easily enough."

My shield was shrinking even faster now, though I was still struggling to balance on the remaining small island, still keeping out of the warming water.

Zippy, of course, was the alias of the person who worked for the company that made the tests and had sold Lindie the math SAT in advance. Annelise, being a reader, would have no trouble coming up with proof of the transaction, which she could then deliver to Harvard—and any other college Lindie might hope to get into after Harvard took back its offer of admission. Annelise had plenty of time. It was only early July.

"You'd . . . really do that, wouldn't you?" Lindie whispered.

Annelise smiled at her. "Well, maybe I don't have to, after all. It all depends on you, Lindie."

Lindie turned slowly to me. I took her hand and faced Annelise. "What's going on?" I asked her, my thin, rocking island so small and unsteady now I was down on my knees, clinging to its edges. "What are you talking about? I don't understand any of this."

Annelise giggled. *Oh, come off it, Jared,* she gloated, flicking away my last shards of protection with no effort at all, like a child romping in slush.

It was Annelise who had melted my shield. She had known all along I could read. I didn't have to hide from her anymore. All the ice was gone anyway.

I hesitated. What would it be like inside Annelise's

venomous mind now that she was a reader? Was it safe to take even a little peek? Probably not.

But I was uncontrollably curious. And I had to try to help Lindie.

I threw myself in.

sixteen

And landed with a bone-jolting thud on a surface like tarmac. The air shimmered; sweat stung my eyes. It was hotter than the beach at noon, but there was no refreshing ocean to cool off in. There didn't seem to be much of anything here except this barren, paved wasteland, like an endless parking lot. Was this the reality of Annelise's mind, or was it a shield?

Suddenly I knew I was being watched, inside and out. But there was no place to hide here and no hope of an ice shield in the blistering heat. I was completely vulnerable and exposed. My heart pounding, I shaded my eyes and looked up.

Into Annelise's gigantic face. It dominated the sky like some bloated primeval sun. Maybe this *wasn't* a shield. It made sense that the primary focus of Annelise's mind would be Annelise.

She smiled, and glorious fiery coronas arched with languid violence millions of miles into space. She was flexing her muscles, testing her strength. Her powers were greater than mine would ever be. I remembered what she had written in her journal about Dee-Dee, the girl who had died because of her: "It wasn't my fault she decided to go out just before that freak squall blew up. . . . The bitch shouldn't have gotten in my way."

I couldn't stand it here. I rushed for the noisy, busy distraction of Grandma's factory.

And was greeted by vast silence. Spiderwebs dangled from the broken, rusting machinery; holes gaped in the ceiling. A few scraps of torn photographs lay half buried in the thick layer of dust on the balcony floor.

I should have known. Grandma wouldn't be allowed to operate on her own anymore. She'd be Annelise's slave now. She had no choice. Annelise had all the information about Grandma's crimes.

And I was a lot weaker than Grandma. Annelise must have already read my journal and explored my mind. What particular information would she use to try to control *me*? I had to find out, or I'd have no hope of resisting her. Shielding my eyes, I jumped back to Annelise's scorching parking lot.

What do you think you're going to do to me, Annelise?

She was happy to answer my question. She blasted me with quotes from my journal—pathetic mushy entries about how much I loved her, my most personal embarrassing fantasies about her. Everyone in the family would know about them. I cringed on the pavement.

And Annelise was so confident of her power that she wasn't even hiding what she would do to Grandma. She would take possession of Grandma's property and whatever money Grandma had as soon as she was of legal age. She would take control of the family, who would not resent her but see her as their kindly benefactress. She wasn't exactly sure yet what Lindie's role in her life would be, except that it would be miserably servile for however long Lindie lived. She wouldn't expose Lindie's secret immediately; she would wield it like an electric cattle prod.

Quotes from her journal kept rolling sickeningly around in my head: "No way I can get out of another deadly summer at the beach, a prison there with the boring, ugly old relatives always around and that loathsome nuisance Amy they'll be expecting me to take care of—I wish she'd just drown and get it over with. . . . Other people I can maybe play some cute little tricks on. Like hunky Bruce over on Indian Neck; hunky and rich—they're the most important family in the neighborhood. . . . Now Eric's sick in bed, a gorgeous shade of vermilion against those tasteless yellow sheets. . . . Poor, sweet Gail made a lot of slashes around her wrists; too bad they found her in time. . . . It's going to be a real spicy summer after all. Having Jared to play with, knowing Bruce and Eric are also slobbering over me. It'll be fun sneaking around them and the whole family, too. Like Jared's father—all I had to do was slip him those two extra triples, and he had no idea Jared and I were sitting right there holding hands. And everybody thinks I'm kindly Miss Perfection meaning nobody any harm. Except for that Harvard cow. But you know me. I'll get something on her. She'll learn."

Annelise's mind was too ugly to take for another instant. And there was something else I needed to know. I tumbled exhaustedly in on Grandma. I wanted the answer to the basic question that was more baffling than ever now: Why had Grandma wanted Annelise to be a reader?

But there was no hint of a clue in the ruined factory, not even any torn photographs now, only endless spiderwebs and dust and dead flies sticking to my sweaty body as I searched the balcony floor. Grandma might be Annelise's slave, but she was still stronger than I was, her shield unbreakable.

But was Grandma's shield also impenetrable to Annelise? I wondered blearily as my mind lurched back into the kitchen.

Lindie was still squeezing my hand; this all had

happened so fast that Lindie was only beginning to notice that nobody was talking.

I looked into her mind. She was terrified; she was bewildered. She didn't know how Annelise had discovered her secret, but she had no doubt Annelise would use it. Yet as much as she had always hated Annelise, I could find only a very small vengeful urge in Lindie to lash back at her. She was in a tough spot, and she wasn't wasting her energy on useless feelings of hostility.

She trusted me more than ever now. It was clear to her that I was no part of Annelise's plan. I squeezed Lindie's hand harder, and we stared at each other for a long moment. Then I dropped her hand, and we both picked up our glasses and drained them.

Lindie took a deep breath and turned to Annelise. "What do you want, Annelise?" she said, and I remembered myself asking Grandma exactly the same question the day before.

"The truth," Annelise said without hesitation. "You take the blame for Amy's almost drowning. The family has to trust me again. I'm sure we can easily convince everybody, since it really was your fault—and I was completely innocent."

Grandma, meanwhile, had whipped the empty beer glasses away and replaced them with full ones. Lindie took a long swallow, staring at Annelise, and I gulped down just as much.

Lindie put down the glass and nodded at Annelise. "Of course," she said evenly. "Just what I'd expect Do you know you're a prisoner? That you're completely controlled by what other people think of you? I thought I hated you, and of course I always will hate you, don't get the wrong idea or anything," she went on, her tone surprisingly conversational. "But now I feel sorry for you more than I hate you."

Annelise smiled, forcing herself with effort to ignore Lindie's remark. We'd be dealing with the rest of the family soon, and Annelise was getting into her role again. "Poor Grandma's the one with the problem, not me," she said pleasantly. "She didn't understand what she saw with her telescope because she wasn't wearing her glasses; everybody knows she's always forgetting where she puts them. She's losing it. All the spiders in her house—yuck!" She moved her chair away from a little gray spider that was skittering toward her across the tabletop.

Lindie and I had almost finished our beers already, but unfortunately I didn't feel the least bit drunk. Lindie didn't seem drunk either. I sniffed deeply at the glass.

And I noticed, for the first time, something oddly familiar about the smell.

"You all remember what really happened now?" Annelise said. "I asked Eric *and* Lindie to keep an eye on Amy, right? Jared was there when I said it; he heard every word. Then everyone else forgot about Amy. I was the one who remembered and saved her. And all of you let me take the blame when Grandma dumped it on me." Annelise turned to Grandma. "You made a terrible mistake today, didn't you, Grandma? And you'll admit it. Otherwise you might have to admit to a few other things." She tilted her head and slid her eyes to the side, folding her hands in front of her. "I'm sure everybody in town would be very interested to hear what you have to say about your friends the Winstons. Of course, because of Jared, all *three* of us already know what you did."

Lindie stared at Grandma, her eyes widening. It was finally sinking in on her that Grandma really *had* robbed the ATM and blackmailed the Winstons.

Grandma hardly reacted at all to Annelise's threat. She only stared blankly at the spider, which had changed course, moving toward Annelise again. I had never seen Grandma so quiet and passive. I darted into her mind another time, to try to find out what she was really thinking and how much she blamed me for what I had suggested to Lindie about her. But there was still only the ruined factory, telling me nothing. Either Grandma was hiding, or she was helpless.

Annelise must have been in the swamp longer than Grandma. She wasn't as clever, but she had more brute power. Did Grandma's uncharacteristic meekness mean she was scared of Annelise? That thought made everything a lot more frightening.

"OK, everybody?" Annelise stood up, wanting to get away from the spider. She strolled to the little mirror beside the sink, patted her hair, checked her expression. "You do what I'm asking, and your little secrets are safe."

Lindie stood up abruptly. "All right!" she snapped.

She was so scared of what Annelise could do to the rest of her life that being hated by the family seemed mild in comparison. She was going along with this because she thought it was only a single incident; she believed that acquiescing now would protect her for good. She had no idea what Annelise's life plan was.

"Good. You're not going to be stupid and waste time. Let's go." Annelise started for the door. Grandma picked up the large canvas bag in which she carried her sunglasses and baby oil and other beach supplies.

"Wait," I said, knocking my chair over as I got to my feet. I just couldn't stand to let Annelise get away with this. And what she had said about "your little secrets" made me realize that she really *didn't* have anything to use against me. So what if the family knew what was in my journal? Stopping Annelise was a lot more important than my own embarrassment. I was the only one without a truly dangerous secret, the only one who could challenge her.

Annelise spun around. "Yes, cousin dear?" she said, smiling at me.

"Please, Annelise, be reasonable," I appealed to her. "Why can't we just say . . . it was everybody's fault? Not one person in particular. We—we all take the blame."

She said nothing, continuing to smile artificially at me. I had to be tougher.

"You know I can't lie, Annelise," I reminded her, trying to keep my voice steady. "You know how—how *pathetic* I am that way. I can't say it was Lindie's fault that Amy almost drowned; *you* were the one who did it on purpose."

I felt a glow of admiration from Lindie—quickly extinguished by a sharp gust of fear.

"But that's not the *truth*, Jared," Annelise said earnestly. "And I know you want to help Lindie," she added. "If you don't do what I want, she'll get axed, and it will all be because of you."

"Please, Jared," Lindie said softly. And I read her, and I saw that as much as Lindie hated what we were being forced to do, she didn't want me to try to resist. Because if I did, then Annelise would get her. Obeying Annelise seemed to Lindie the lesser of two evils.

I picked up the chair and slowly set it in place.

"Your little fit is over, Jared? You're ready to go along with the *truth?* Good." Annelise studied me for a moment, considering my problem with lying. "You don't have to say much, you know. Just nod and agree with what Lindie and Grandma say and look sheepish. That should come naturally to you. Let's go."

Annelise briskly opened the door; we stepped outside.

seventeen

And there was the sparkling sand, the waves rolling against the rocks, the members of our devoted family relaxing on the beach. There was also another boy, very tanned and good-looking in his cutoff jeans, sitting next to Eric. Bruce, nephew of the Winstons, whose family was the most important and influential in the neighborhood. Were we going to go ahead with Annelise's plan, even with him around?

We started toward the others. Amy ran to meet us, her round face pink and beaming with happiness underneath her short white blond hair. Soon Annelise would be trusted to take care of Amy again.

Annelise knelt and hugged Amy. I marveled that she had the nerve to get anywhere near Amy in sight of the others, after what had happened. But it was just what an innocent person would do. It was a logical first step.

Amy nodded, wide-eyed, as Annelise pressed her cheek against Amy's for quite a long time. Finally Annelise stood up and took Amy's hand, and we began walking again.

Bruce beamed at Annelise, and she smiled back at him. But the people in our family were studiously not looking at us, out of embarrassment as well as shock and anger at what Annelise had done.

Except for Aunt Grace, who was squeezing the arms of her beach chair, her eyes on Annelise and Amy.

Annelise knew how they all felt, and she couldn't stand it. Her toleration of their attitude toward her was reaching its limit; the burning coals were blistering her. They had to see her as charming and kind and trustworthy again, and it had to happen right away. "Hurry, Lindie and Grandma!" she whispered. "Tell them!"

But before Grandma or Lindie could say anything, Aunt Grace got up from her chair and strolled over to Amy and Annelise. "Why don't you just come over here with me, honey?" Aunt Grace said as she carefully disengaged Amy's hand from Annelise's, not looking at Annelise.

"What's the matter, Mommy?" Amy said, confused.

"Annelise is too busy to play with you anymore," Aunt Grace explained.

"But Annelise is my friend," Amy protested.

"Just stay away from her," Aunt Grace said, and everybody but Amy knew she was really speaking to Annelise. Aunt Grace put her arms on Amy's shoulders and moved her back toward her chair.

Everyone was staring at Annelise. "But Aunt Grace, you don't . . . ," Annelise said woefully, watching her beloved Amy being taken away from her. Then she bravely straightened her shoulders and wiped her eyes, hurt and innocent. "Please, Grandma. Please, Lindie," she appealed to them. "How can you go on . . . letting them think—"

"Letting them think what?" Uncle George said, eyeing Grandma and Lindie suspiciously. He was Annelise's father; he hadn't liked seeing her take the blame for what happened to Amy.

Grandma said nothing. She seemed paralyzed. Lindie knew she had to act now, or else Annelise would carry out her threats. She took a deep breath and marched over to Aunt Grace. "I'm—I'm sorry about what happened to Amy today," Lindie began.

And even though I knew the consequences, I couldn't bear to watch Lindie do it.

Wait, Lindie! Stop! I mentally cried out, so upset that I forgot she couldn't hear me.

Bruce was embarrassed about this family scene, but he was also curious, turning to look at Annelise, then back to Grandma and Lindie. Neither of them spoke.

Annelise was in so much pain now from what the others were thinking about her that she just couldn't wait. "Don't you remember, Grandma?" Annelise said gently. "You didn't see what really happened with Amy because you weren't wearing your glasses when—when you were watching through the telescope. You told us that just now, in the house."

"Did I, Annelise?" Grandma said, her face expressionless.

Annelise was boiling inside, her mind so scalding I could barely get near it. But she still had enough control not to let it show on the surface. "Yes, you did, Grandma," she said, like a little child reminding a parent of a promise. "And . . . you also told me about your visits to the Winstons' house."

Grandma coughed and put her hand to her mouth, almost dropping her beach bag. She didn't seem to be expecting such a direct attack.

"What are you talking about, Annelise?" Aunt Maggie wanted to know. "Mother never visits the Winstons. Everybody knows how much she—" Then she remembered Bruce and stopped in midsentence.

"Hates them, Aunt Maggie?" Annelise finished for her in a small voice, giving the impression that she was merely being honest and straightforward about a difficult subject. "I didn't say she visited the Winstons. I said she visited their *house*." She turned to Bruce. "I think it's really sad that your aunt and uncle decided to sell," she said, as though she meant it. "Do *you* know why they're doing it?"

He shrugged and lifted his hands. "They say they're nervous now, because of the break-in. We keep telling them they're overreacting. I mean, nobody was hurt. Nothing valuable was taken. But they're afraid of something." He turned and looked at Grandma.

"Grandma's so smart, and she's always watching them with her telescope. Maybe she knows something about it," Annelise suggested.

"Hold on a minute," said Uncle George, who was so eager to see Annelise vindicated, and the blame shunted elsewhere, that he didn't care that Bruce was there. "We're getting off the subject. What were you going to say about Amy, Lindie?"

"It *was* Annelise who saved her life," Aunt Beatrice put in.

Aunt Grace was squinting at Lindie now. "Go on, Lindie," she said impatiently. "You're acting so funny. What's the matter?"

"I'm sorry, Aunt Grace," Lindie mumbled again, looking miserable, and she sighed. But she had to protect Grandma and herself.

Annelise had won. Her eyes were fixed on Lindie, her mouth twitching as though she were trying not to gloat. And how perfect for her that Bruce was there, as an added threat to Grandma and to make sure these secrets could not be kept in the family.

"Well, Lindie?" Aunt Grace prodded her.

But Lindie didn't answer. There was a look of wonderment on her face as she turned to me.

Don't be so afraid, Jared, a sort of voice lilted like music inside my head. Not Annelise's voice. Not Grandma's voice.

And then I knew what Lindie and I had really been drinking.

eighteen

Our house was beside a river.

It wasn't like Grandma's elaborate constructions. There was nowhere to hide anything here. The place was hardly more than a covered porch, with comfortable mats on the bare plank floor. The river flowed past, sunlight and tree shadows rippling over the surface.

This place was a refuge for Lindie and me, with no traps or shields. In a billionth of a second Lindie knew everything I did, about the swamp water.

about Annelise, about Grandma. She understood it all.

We had *drunk* the swamp water, not just been briefly dunked in it. Naturally its effects would be more potent.

"Maybe I should go," Bruce was saying. But he wasn't moving. Nobody had told him that Amy had almost drowned, but he knew *something* had happened, and he was very eager to find out exactly what was going on. He was also extremely interested in what Grandma had to do with his aunt and uncle's problems.

Lindie and I hovered above and below and in the middle of the rest of the world, which seemed to be as transparent as glass. We felt the glow of Amy's love for Annelise. We experienced the varying degrees of tension felt by everyone else in the family, and Bruce's increasing curiosity. We knew what the worried real-estate agent was saying to the people looking at the Winstons' house, who were insisting that the price was too high. We felt the primitive, jagged excitement of a cat three houses away that had cornered a terrified mouse. We heard Karen, the cabin attendant in the little plane two thousand feet above the beach, telling the passengers to fasten their seat belts for landing. She wasn't thinking about what she was saying; she was thinking about her boyfriend, Mitch, in Boston.

But most of all, we were aware of Annelise's desperate need to fix her image.

It was wonderful to be able to see so much. But we were frightened by what Grandma had done. She must have diluted the swamp water with beer, but it was still highly toxic stuff she had been dumping down our throats. Sure, it was logical that drinking it would give us even more special powers. But it was also logical that it could kill us. Was her intention to wipe us out or to help us? And if she wanted to help us, how did she know it was safe to do it this way?

There was only one way she could be sure. She had already been drinking large quantities of swamp water herself. We knew at once that this was so. We knew it precisely because we could *not* see the answer in Grandma's mind.

We stood on the vibrating balcony of her factory. We could see everything in a lot more detail than I had before. The old knitting machines, shiny again, clashed in intricate patterns below us, producing yards and yards of delicate silvery weblike fabric; the tireless spiders, responding to nods from Grandma, scurried to keep the machines oiled and polished. With our heightened powers, we sensed that there was a message, a plan, being woven into the fabric.

But we couldn't read it. Only if Grandma's power were superior to ours would she be able to hide anything from us. She smiled in approval at our deduction. And then she was gone. She would *never* allow us to see everything.

But Annelise, tiny Annelise, who had been given no big dose of swamp water to drink, was powerless to shield anything from us. We could read her completely. I had been wrong about the burning coals.

Our image of Annelise changed, becoming clearer and more complex.

I had already figured, with Grandma's help, that Annelise's insatiable need for admiration was where she was vulnerable. But now we were so far above her we understood how fragile and weak it made her. She was more pitiful than Lindie had realized. She had no concept of friendship; her journal was her only confidante, and that was why she told it so much. Other people existed only to bolster the delicate mirror of her self-image. And if the support of their admiration was taken away, the mirror would warp, and become distorted and ugly, and eventually shatter—like a picture window bursting in a hurricane. Annelise would do anything to keep that from happening.

We understood her weakness now, and we had a lot of ideas about how to use it. But Grandma was faster.

"Oh, don't go, Bruce," Annelise was saying. She wanted this scene to be as publicly humiliating to Lindie as possible.

"Yes, please stay, Bruce," Grandma said, suddenly breaking out of her paralysis and becoming her usual animated self again. She set down her beach bag and pulled a sheaf of papers out of it. "I have something fascinating for *everybody*."

Annelise didn't like the way Grandma was interrupting Lindie's confession. Annelise's mirror, already crooked and unsteady, began to tremble. "Excuse me, Grandma. Could you wait with that stuff until

Lindie finishes? Then we can talk about the Winstons," she said in a sweet, condescending tone, shooting a silent threat at Grandma.

"But you don't understand, darling," Grandma said. "Everything that matters is right here." She waved the sheaf of papers in the fresh ocean breeze.

"Oh, Grandma, what *is* all that?" Annelise said, a trace of impatience showing in her voice.

"Never you mind," Grandma said. "Believe me, everyone will get a kick out of it."

The mirror began to rock dangerously, its reflection of Annelise distorted now, one side of her mouth bulging up almost to her eye, her nose and nostrils widening in a snoutlike way. "But . . . ," Annelise said, "but you couldn't have—"

"Yes, dear, I copied your notebook," Grandma breezily told her.

In the mirror, Annelise screamed.

"Annelise left this notebook on the porch yesterday," Grandma began.

"It's just creative writing, from school! And I didn't leave it there. Grandma stole it from our house." Annelise looked frantically from one person to another, breathing hard. She was making a monumental effort to ignore her grotesque, piggish face in the mirror. "Grandma stole Jared's notebook, too. She used them to blackmail us to get something she wanted—just the way she stole something from the Winstons and blackmailed them to sell their house." She turned on me, knowing I couldn't lie. "Right, Jared?"

Suddenly everybody's attention was focused on me.

"Oh, come off it, Annelise," I said confidently. "I saw you leave that notebook on Grandma's porch yesterday. Grandma didn't steal our notebooks or blackmail anybody. She never said anything about visiting the Winstons. Why do you keep making things up? Everybody already knows you lied about Eric."

Of course, the family believed me. They knew I couldn't lie.

So why *was* I suddenly lying so easily now? There could only be one answer: Drinking the swamp water had given me this ability.

Like the rest of the family, Annelise didn't know that. She stood frozen in place, too horrified to think of what to do.

"Naturally I opened the notebook, not knowing what it was," Grandma went on explaining to the others, walking toward Aunt Grace, her hands busy with the papers. "As soon as I read a page, I knew it was my *duty* to make copies, to share it with everybody else." She thrust a sheet of paper at Aunt Grace. "Here, Grace. You'll just *love* this part about Amy."

"Mother!" Uncle George protested. "If that's something personal of Annelise's, you better just stop this foolishness and give it to me." Uncle George wanted to read it, of course, but he didn't want anybody else to.

Grandma shrugged. "It's just fiction—according to Annelise."

Aunt Grace frowned, not taking the paper. "But still, I'm not sure it's right to . . . uh . . ."

"Oh, come *on*, Grace!" Grandma said, with a throaty conspiratorial chuckle. "I know you're dying of curiosity." She dropped the paper in Aunt Grace's lap.

And Aunt Grace grabbed it quickly, before the wind blew it away, and began to read.

"Here, Eric. This one's for you," Grandma said brightly, handing him a sheet. "And Bruce! What a lucky coincidence I made an extra copy of *this* page, where she writes about you and what she did to Dee-Dee."

Of course, Bruce would tell everyone in the neighborhood about Annelise's journal. Grandma turned away from him, waving the papers again. "George and Beatrice! Have I got a bundle of goodies for *you* two!"

Annelise's mirror exploded, her self-image splintering into a million knifelike shards of glass. "She's lying! It's a fake! She wrote it herself!" Annelise shouted, rushing toward Grandma to try to stop her from giving copies of her journal to her parents.

"If it's a fake, then what are you so upset about, dear?" Grandma asked her, whipping the papers into Uncle George's hand. Annelise grabbed for them, but Uncle George was a lot bigger than she was and held them out of her reach, reading as he did so.

"But Grandma and Lindie, they—they . . ." Annelise's voice faded. There was nothing she could do. Her threats against Grandma and Lindie were useless now. Her journal would confirm how sick and dangerous she was. No one would ever believe a word she said again.

Uncle George, Bruce, Eric, and Aunt Grace were reading Grandma's specially selected pages of the journal avidly. And Annelise, too upset to shield herself, was being sliced by their outrage and repugnance. She just couldn't take the pain. She stumbled in a confused zigzag path across the sand, trying to escape from their thoughts. Her worried mother went after her; her father kept on reading.

Grandma, Lindie, and I were part of the action on the beach; we also watched it from a vast distance.

Thanks for the beer, Grandma.

My pleasure.

The three of us were thinking about what it was going to be like for Annelise now. Her parents would probably send her to some school for criminally disturbed teenagers, a highly disciplinary place where her every move would be watched. She would almost certainly be under psychiatric care, which she would detest. And being a reader, she would be constantly slashed by the terrible things people were thinking about her.

Will she ever get better? Lindie wondered.

Maybe, Grandma told us, and vanished into her factory.

Lindie and I were alone together in our open house by the river. We had all the time we wanted. We could fix it so ten hours went by in our own world while only a nanosecond passed on the beach.

But we weren't relaxing. As much as we disliked Annelise, we were worried about the suffering she was in for now. We would be very clearly aware of her pain, because of our special powers. It would hurt, we would try to avoid it as much as we could, but we still probably wouldn't be able to resist sneaking in and taking an occasional peek at what she was going through. We also knew we'd have to be dealing with the shock waves in the family for months to come, and that would be no fun at all.

At the same time, we couldn't help feeling pretty smug.

Because of our superabilities, we would have no problem hiding our relationship from the rest of the family. Our lives, stretching out endlessly, would be whatever we chose to make them. We didn't know exactly how much power we had, only that we had a tremendous amount of it. There seemed to be almost no limit to our ability to read people.

But we knew we had to monitor ourselves. We had to remember Annelise. If we forgot, we could become more dangerous than she had been. After all, Lindie had committed fraud with her SATs. . . .

And you lied, Jared, Lindie reminded me. *I mean, it was for a good cause. But it was still the first time you ever lied.*

I know. I've got to . . . think about that.

It was a lucky thing there were two of us, two minds together more alert than one, each of us there to keep the other from slipping. Not allowing our power to corrupt us was really our only problem.

Wrong, Grandma cackled.

She was right, as always. We *did* have another problem.

Grandma had drunk more swamp water than either of us; she had more power than we did. And Grandma was plenty smart. To rub it in, she pulled us deeper into her factory.

Machines rumbled and clanged. And now we could read part of the information stitched into the weblike pattern of the fabric, the older fabric, already woven and fed out of the machines. The patterns told us that for the last month Grandma had known about the boating accident, and Eric's sunburn, and Annelise's obsession with other people's opinions. Grandma had searched for a way to protect people from Annelise, especially me and Lindie, her favorites.

The pattern changed as we moved along toward the machines, studying the fabric, keeping away from Grandma's spider employees. Here the weaving was irregular, unsure. This was where Grandma had taken a risk. She had gambled that putting Annelise in the swamp, making her painfully aware of what people were really thinking about her, would cripple her—as soon as her journal went public. She wasn't sure it would work.

But the gamble had paid off. The fabric became tight and orderly again. We read about how part of Grandma's plan had been to make us stronger than Annelise by secretly feeding us swamp water. If Annelise ever tried to use her powers in a dangerous or malicious way again, we'd be able to outmaneuver her. That would keep her in check. In this way Grandma had prevented Annelise from wrecking many lives, as she otherwise would have done without any special power at all.

We approached the noisy machines and craned our necks to see the fabric that was now being woven. We didn't dare get too close to those plunging needles. But we were near enough to see that *this* new pattern was illegible to us. Not only was it unfinished, but it was in another language; we could read no information in it at all. At least we were smart enough to understand why. This was the part she was still working on, the part that hadn't happened yet. She would *never* allow us to know anything about that.

She dropped us from the booming factory back into the peacefulness of our house. Crickets chirped; water lapped gently in the evening hush. Soon it would be night.

Was Grandma's factory her real self, or was it just a game she was playing with us? We didn't know. But at least she did seem to be on the right side. The patterns she had allowed us to read were basically good things she had accomplished.

But her methods were not exactly humane. There must have been a less punishing and vindictive way to stop Annelise. Grandma hadn't asked our permission to feed us swamp water. And the other things she had done—robbing the ATM, blackmailing the Winstons—were far from benevolent. We realized that she had somehow kept that part of the old fabric hidden from us. Grandma was ruthless and amoral, and she was in control.

And now the serenity of our house trembled like the darkening surface of the river, as we realized how much we *didn't* know. The ATM cards, for instance. Just picking the numbers from people's brains wasn't enough to rob the bank. How had she gotten the cards away from people without their being aware of it right away? It was also suspiciously convenient that Bruce had been there on the beach today, to spread the news about Annelise. And then there was the question of the swamp water: How had Grandma known it was safe to drink it? And why *wasn't* it poisonous? We didn't have a clue.

OK, we had power. What we didn't have was protection from Grandma.

But we both felt Grandma's attention was elsewhere for the moment. "How much do you think she can do?" Lindie whispered, glancing around, hoping Grandma couldn't hear us.

"Almost anything," I whispered back, feeling as tense as Lindie about this conversation. "I wonder what her next move is going to be."

"Do you think there's any way we can hide from her or try to protect ourselves?"

"There might be," I said apprehensively. "I mean, she can't be constantly spying on us every minute. There's only one of her, after all. So maybe we can—"

Suddenly we sensed skittering above us, a tiny

noise, and jumped nervously up from the floor mats. Then we laughed. It was only a little spider, busily weaving a silvery web up in the rafters.

That was a relief.